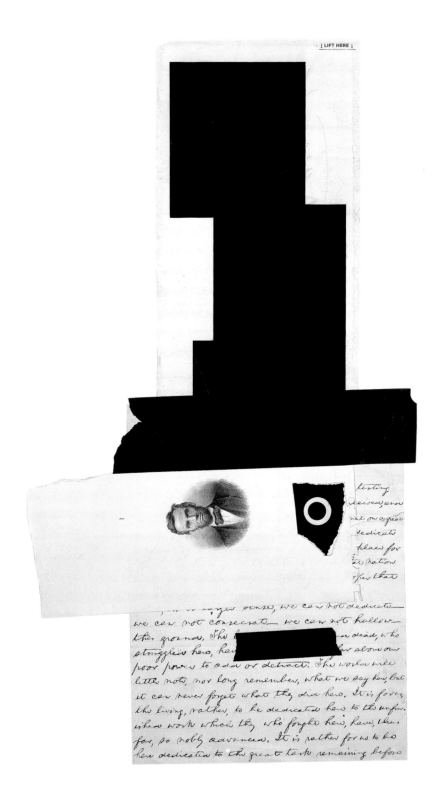

Dascillus, cervinus Lam Curtis

Anysoncha, cervina,

Atopa Cryptorsarbretus, cervina Rupt

oblonga; obscure fusca, carea pilis tenuissimis obsita   Dumer 1826

Chrysomela.

4

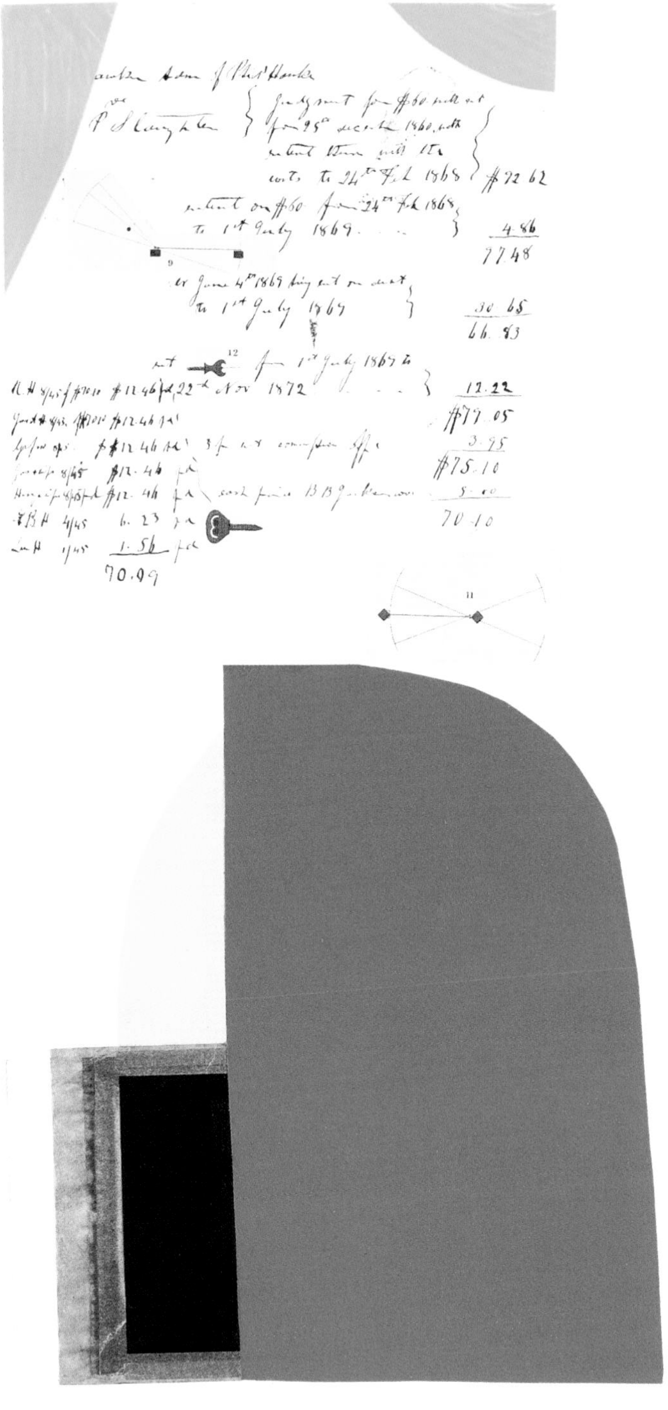

$92.62
4.86
77.48
30.65
66.83
12
12.22
$77.05
3.95
$75.10
5.00
70.10
70.09
9
11

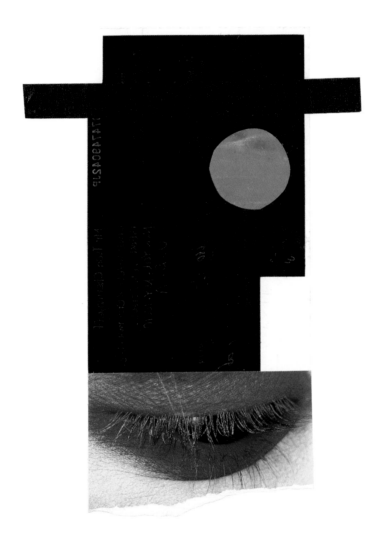

Suspects, Smokers, Soldiers, and Salesladies

Collages by Ivan Chermayeff

Essay by Joseph Giovannini

Lars Müller Publishers

The author wishes to thank those who have been
supportive of his collages, especially, Roger Ricco and
Frank Maresca of the Ricco/Maresca Gallery in New York,
David Floria of the David Floria Gallery in Aspen,
Gayle Maxon-Edgerton of the Gerald Peters Gallery in
Santa Fe, the master printer Jon Cone of Cone Editions
and Craig O'Brien of O'Brien Graphics. The assistance
of Lori Shepard, Patsy Madden and Frank Dylla of
Chermayeff & Geismar is much appreciated as is the advice,
concern and counsel of publisher Lars Müller. Finally, many
thanks to Joseph Giovannini for his thoughtful and sensitive
essay and to my inhouse critics, my wife Jane Clark Chermayeff
and my son, Sam Chermayeff.

Colorseparations: Ast & Jakob AG, Köniz
Printing: Stämfli AG, Berne
Binding: Buchbinderei Burkhardt AG, Mönchaltorf

Printed in Switzerland

Distributed in North America by
Princeton Architectural Press, New York
All other countries:
Birkhäuser Publishers, Basel, Switzerland

Lars Müller Publishers
5401 Baden/Switzerland
books@lars-muller.ch

1st Edition 2001
© 2001 Lars Müller Publishers

ISBN 3-907078-38-3

On Making Collages: An Introduction

Can I just talk about seeing? Collages are my notes about observations. They are memories of gathering after a lifelong search for stuff which is visually interesting for one reason or another, believing at the time that I can perhaps use it someday.

My first step in the process of making collages is akin to cooking. No meal is going to be delicious unless the ingredients used are very good. Without onions and garlic, butter and olive oil, fresh fish or good meat and the appropriate herbs and spices, no tasty dish can be concocted.

Once the main ingredients are assembled, I can cut and slice, tear and manipulate the pieces after I have made choices about where a particular collage is going to go.

There are plenty of decisions to make and many endless possibilities to avoid.

The assembly of lots of anything looks good whether they're exactly the same thing or slightly different. Fruit and vegetable stands can only be surpassed by wagon loads of fruits and vegetables. A school of fish, a flight of geese, a constellation of stars, a bag of marbles, loose nails, orchards and allées, fields of pumpkins, beaches of pebbles. Collection becomes provocative, as well as poignant when the objects were not meant to be collected. Suddenly the collection becomes a new totality.

After assembling comes the search for new connections. The power that the elements have on each other changes meanings or builds them.

Friends and places bring images to mind, on the other hand, seeing similarities sometimes forces a direction to be taken. Often I am provoked by common threads of color or size. There is something demanding about the discovery that two seemingly disparate images have a common dimension or are the same color. Then the images come together without further help.

Assembly is juxtaposition, bringing together the unfriendly; joining those images which usually never meet or talk to each other.

Assembling is joining. When the marriage takes, the joints disappear. Sometimes the successful assembly comes from friendships made when the chance meeting of images seems natural, and is taken for granted.

In printed ephemera or fragments lie other qualities. Beyond colors and textures are densities and smoothness and roughness. For me there is a certain magic in, for instance, black. Carbon paper black, painted black, and printed black are different from each other. When they are suddenly brought together the differences become apparent and benefit the collage.

Other qualities come into existence when images are transferred, or screened, or layered, or partially erased, or smudged.

Handwriting is not the same as typeset letters. Writing suggests immediacy, hence freshness. It comes from the writers' own hand, with no typesetter in the background and no competitive graphic character introduced by a typeface.

Writing may be calligraphy or it may not. It may be just plain handwriting with all the inevitable knots and warts and idiosyncrasies. Calligraphy, being the art of beautiful writing, may be too contrived, too worked over, and, in the final result forced and constipated, exactly the opposite of fresh and free, like a characterless singer who has no gravel in the voice.

Of course handwriting must have character. Be legible enough, loose enough, raw and full of gravel.

What about seeing several things repeated? Repeating is an act that forces one to view the act instead of the actor. If something ugly is repeated and remains ugly, it only means that it has not been repeated often enough. Repeating is like enlarging in this respect, because if something ugly is big, then it only means that it was not made big enough. The Saint Louis arch is horrendous as an airport souvenir and quite magnificent as the gateway to the city.

Postage stamps sent through the mails, canceled with post marks, juxtaposed with names and addresses and special little stickers or notes of instruction to the post office come together sometimes with typewriter written labels, sometimes with handwriting.

Air mail in foreign languages with abstract airplanes are never placed on an envelope exactly the same way. Frequently stamps are repeated. Many of the same denomination together makes a visually interesting quality.

Supermarket shelves prove that the visual repetition of the worst possible packages can be a delight, which sometimes even surpasses the repetition of the best packages.

Writing and repeating are both forms of graphic disguise, hiding weak words or dubious designs. Whether or not the intention is deception or distraction or whether the design or arrangement of the elements on an envelope is considered consciously matters little. The act has been made. The elements are on the envelope where they can be seen in a new light. What country does a communication come from? Do I know who sent it?

Between labels and letterforms and language other relationships emerge. The addressee may be a nose, a stamp, an eye.

What is missing? When the label of the sender become an ear or a nose, the addition of yet another element, defines an eye.

The extraordinary fact is that, if a collage presents two eyes, then the nose and the mouth in the right places complete the face. Under these circumstances tremendous liberties can be taken. The mouth and the nose can be something else quite distant. An insect, a pebble, a row of white dots, a line, a piece of tape, all can be a mouth.

How and in what position these disparate elements are placed makes them come together as a face, friendly or dangerous, male or female, funny or peculiar, old or young.

The how is often related to cutting with scissors. Or tearing between fingers. Cutting is clean and sharp and fast. It leaves behind a form that reveals itself clearly, for better or worse. If for worse, one can cut again. Cut paper edges contrast with torn edges and when together each exaggerates the quality of the other. Torn edges are much harder to control and so they're much slower to make in spite of their faster appearance. Scissors are extensions of fingers. Tearing is between fingers. Tearing takes something away- cutting takes away too, but one's watching what's left. A tear is like a brushstroke. Cutting is more like carving. Cutting is drawing, tearing is painting. Both cutting and tearing are fast.

And fast is fresh!

Punching holes or applying dots is a way of making the symbols of images.

Punching and dotting are often a part of the process of making a collage, at least my process.

Punching makes a hole. A hole in a form can give form meaning. Punched holes are eye sockets, nostrils, mouths. Mostly, punches are negative spaces, areas taken away, to see through only occasionally to fill up with something else. Sometimes holes appear to be added, even if they are taken away. That is when holes become buttons and dials, snowflakes and rain, freckles and moles. Then punching becomes dotting, because dotting is adding. Punching is mechanical and round. Dotting can be round but usually isn't because dots are not usually mechanical. Dots are mostly bigger or smaller than punches.

The same dot can mean a worm hole in an apple, an apple, or an apple tree, depending on whether it's black or red, red on green or green on green. Random yellow dots on green are daffodils or dandelions. If they are not random, white dots on black are lights, or, if all in a random row, teeth.

Of course, all dots can change their meanings or lose them. It is possible to have real green apples, but if one wants dots to mean apples, then they must be red. Green dots are not apples. Red dots may also be tomatoes, but not in trees. Neither are yellow dots bananas. Blue dots are nothing but eyes, blueberries and blue flowers, if they're in the right places. Dots are fickle.

Collage makes it possible for everything to be something else.

Ivan Chermayeff

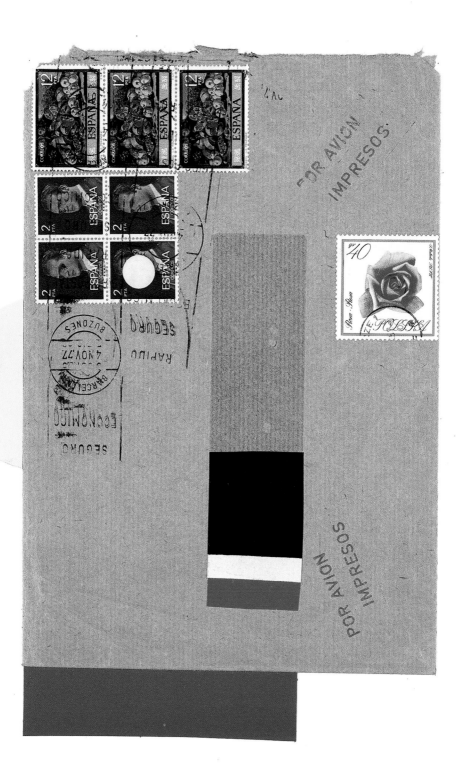

18

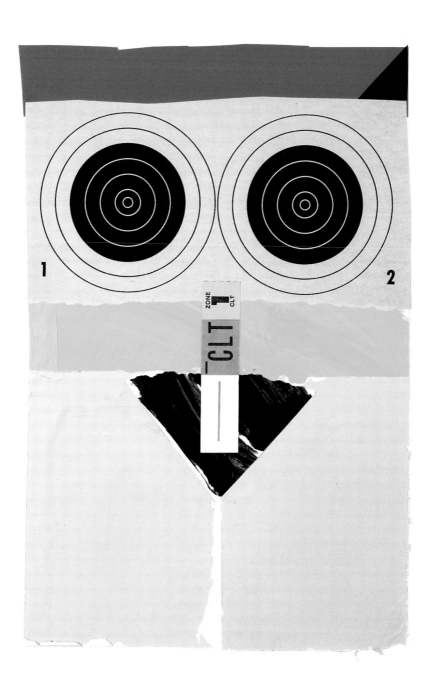

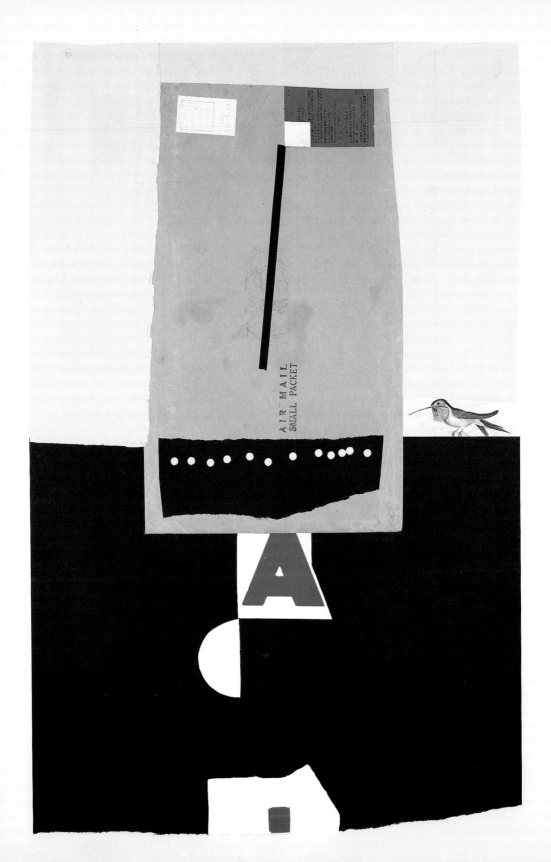

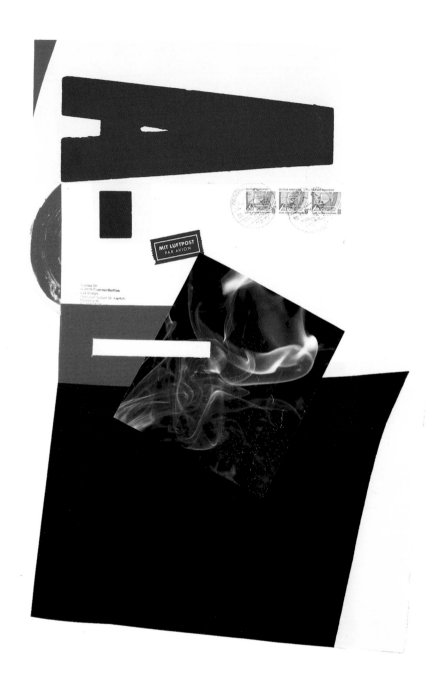

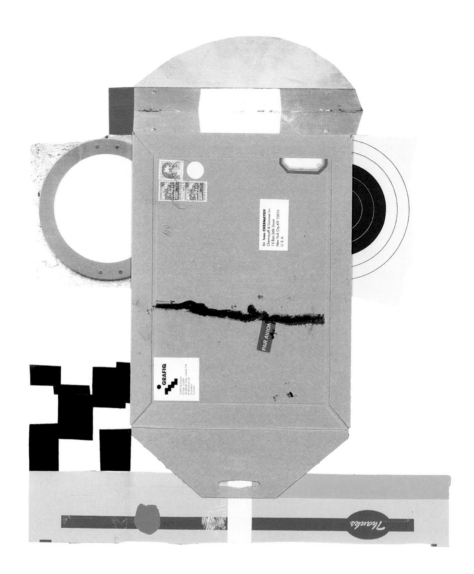

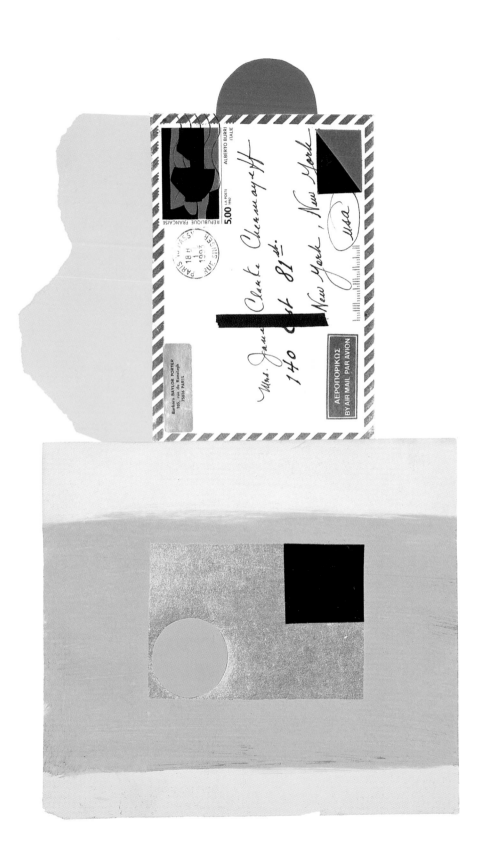

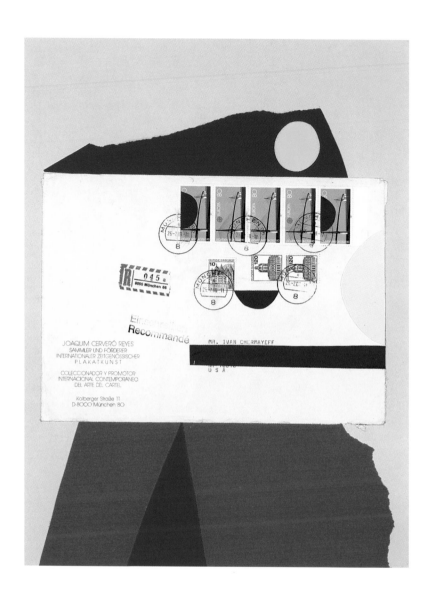

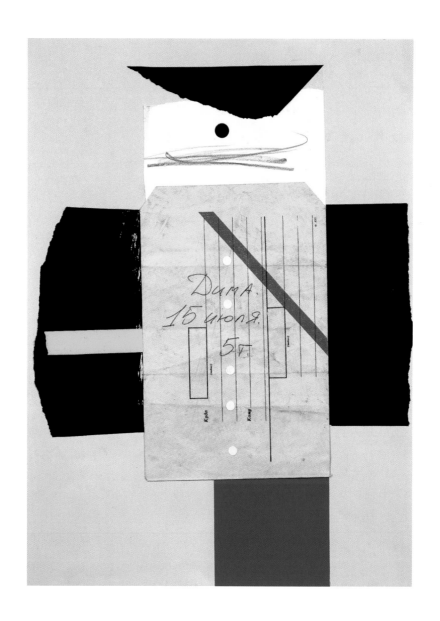

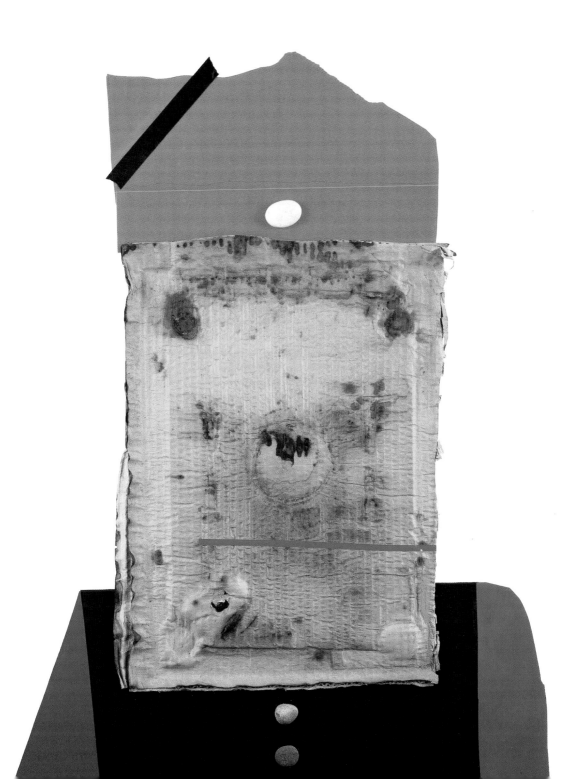

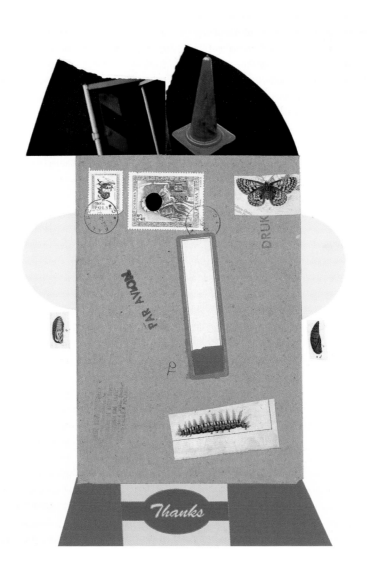

By air mail
Par avion

AIR MAIL

IVAN + JANE CHERMAYEFF.

CHERMAYEFF + GEISMAR ASSOCIATES

15 EAST 26TH ST,

NEW YORK CITY

NY 10010

U.S.A.

PAR AVION

To the attention of Ivan Chermayeff

AIRMAIL

USA

Chermayeff & Geismar Associates
15 East 26 th Street
New-York, NY 10010

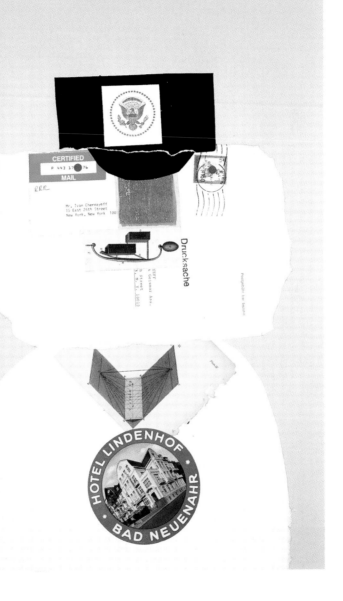

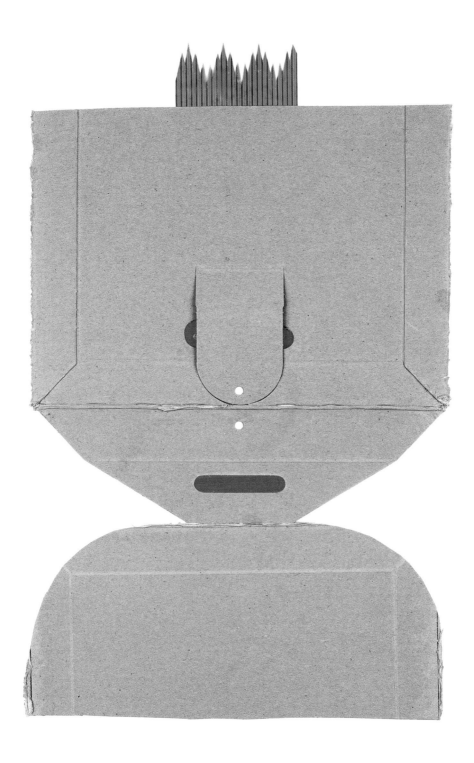

Remite: E. Flores
Antonio Plaza No. 23
Santa Marta La Ribera,
Morelia — Michoacán
58090

Do Not Bend
Favor: No Doblar

VIA AEREA
VIA AEREA
VIA AEREA
VIA AEREA

CORREO AEREO

Air Mail

Charmayel Zvi ... Att. office 15 East 26th Street, New York 10010

Всесоюзное художественно-
производственное объединение
им. Е. В. Вучетича

Приложение № 3
к Правилам приема на ко-
миссию произведений искус-
ства, выполненных до 1945 г.,
и предметов антиквариата.

Художественный салон-
выставка № _____

Форма № 96

0903136

ТОВАРНЫЙ
ЯРЛЫК №   506947

Принято на комиссию « _17_ »   _06_   19 _94_ г.
Дата проведения аукциона « _17_ »   _06_   19 _94_ г.

ХАРАКТЕРИСТИКА ПРОИЗВЕДЕНИЯ

Плотная вставка, галочка
27,4 х 23,7 потеря, дом

Стартовая цена   *Сто пятьдесят*
Аукционная цена   *тыс руб*

Приемщик _____   Комитент
          (подпись)

УЦЕНКА

	Акт №	Дата	Новая цена	Материально ответ-ственное лицо
1				
				(подпись)
			(цена прописью)	
	Акт №	Дата	Новая цена	Материально-ответ-ственное лицо
2				
				(подпись)
			(цена прописью)	
	Акт №	Дата	Новая цена	Материально-ответ-ственное лицо
3				
				(подпись)

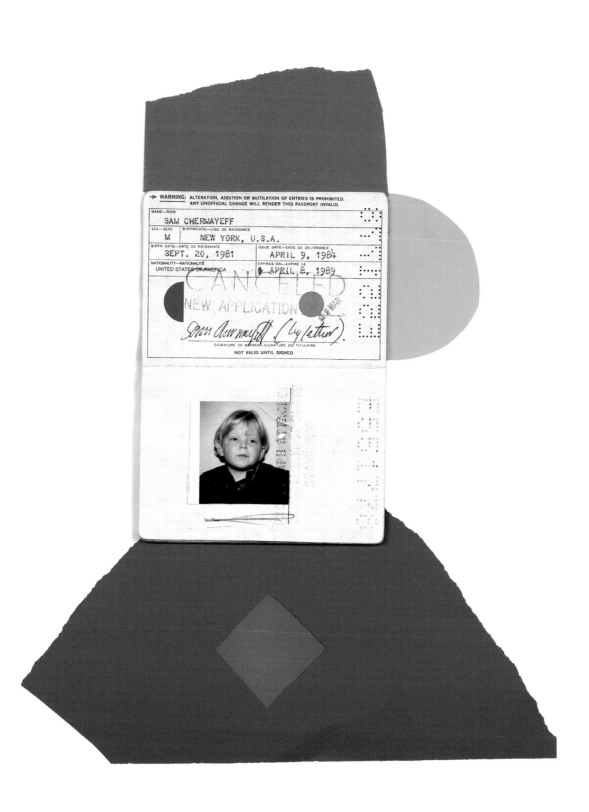

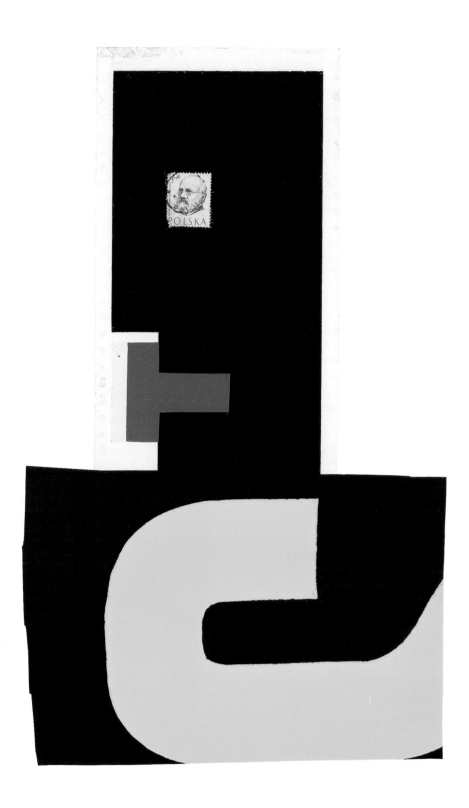

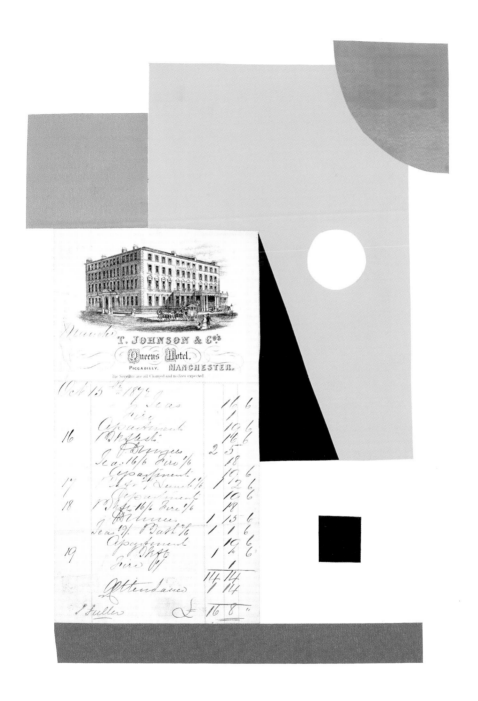

T. JOHNSON & Co's
Queens Hotel.
PICCADILLY.   MANCHESTER.

The Servants are all Charged and no fees expected

Oct 15th 1872	Teas			16	6
	Apartment		1	10	6
16	Breakfast			16	6
	Dinners		2	5	
	Tea 16/6 Fire 1/6			18	
	Apartment		1	12	6
17	Tea & Lunch 1/6				
	Apartment		1	0	6
18	Bkfts 16/6 Fire 1/6			18	
	Dinners		1	15	6
	Teas &c Bath 1/6		1	1	6
	Apartment		1	10	6
19	Bkfts				
	Fire 1/			1	
			14	14	
	Attendance		1	14	
J Fuller		£	16	8	"

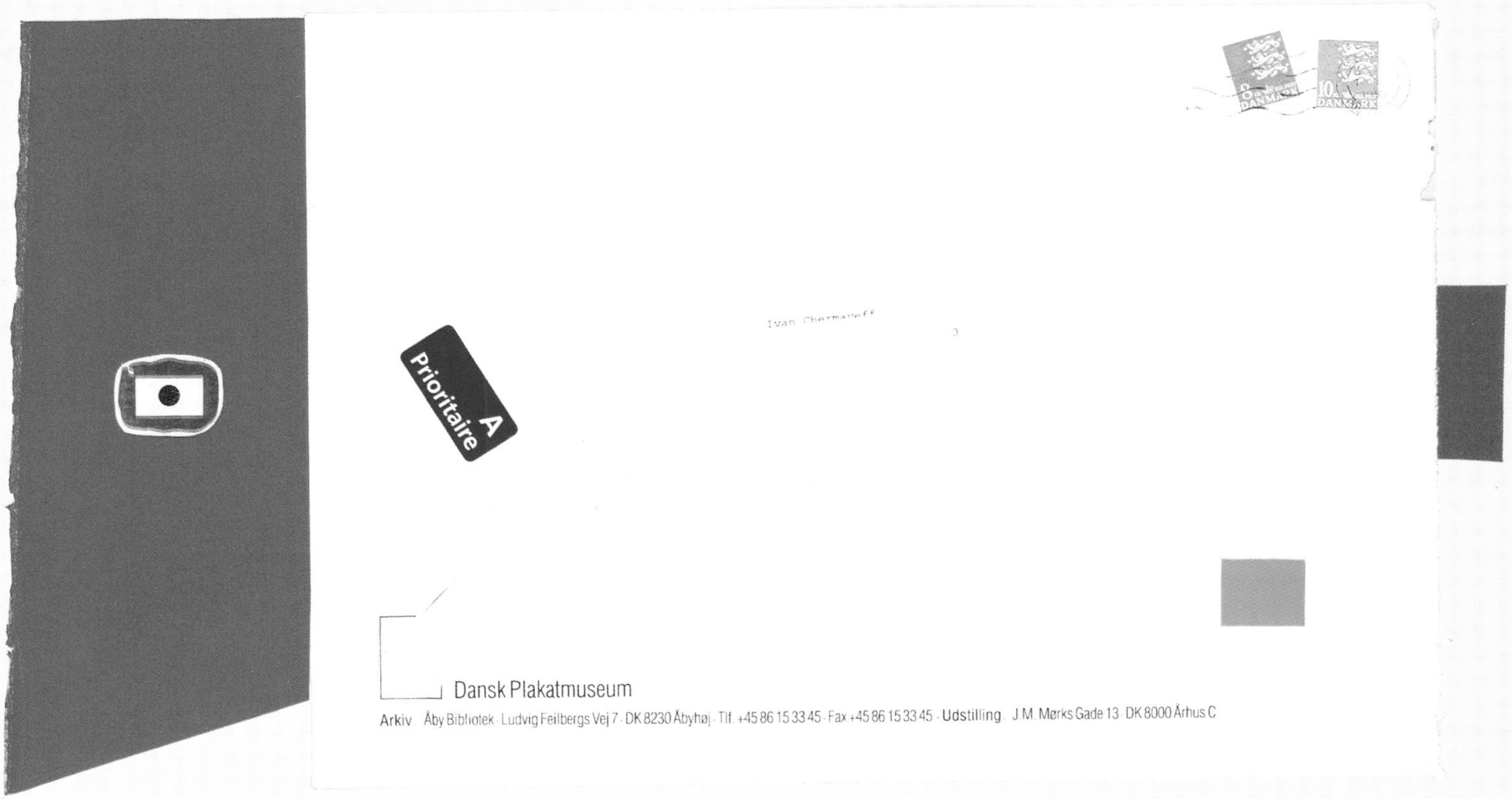

Ivan Chermayeff

Dansk Plakatmuseum

Arkiv Aby Bibliotek Ludvig Feilbergs Vej 7 DK 8230 Åbyhøj Tlf +45 86 15 33 45 Fax +45 86 15 33 45 Udstilling J M. Mørks Gade 13 DK 8000 Århus C

A
Prioritaire

54

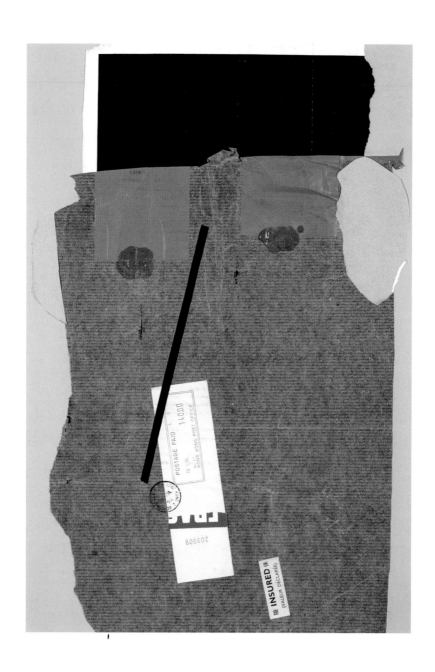

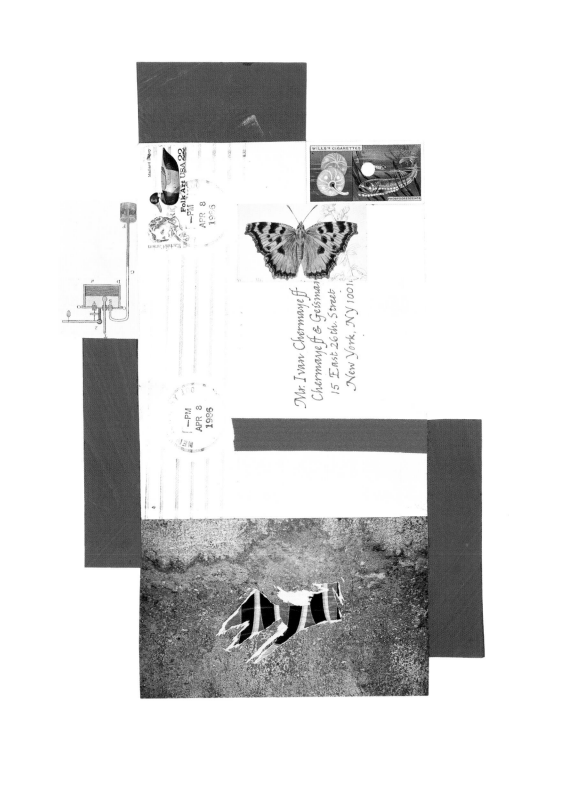

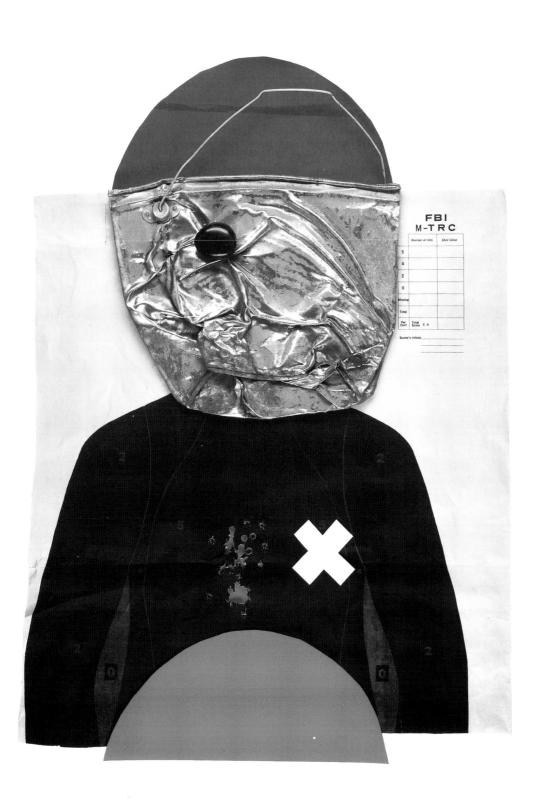

FBI
M-TRC

62

СПРАВКА – CERTIFICATE № СПЖ 188151

2-й экземпляр
Ф. № 377

наименование банковского
утреждения

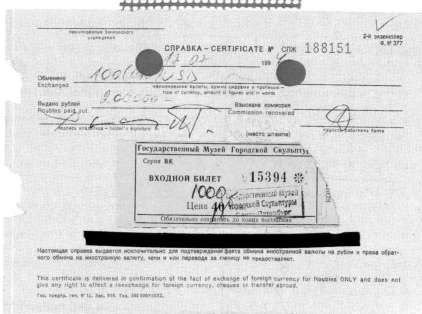

Обменено
Exchanged

наименование валюты, сумма цифрами и прописью –
type of currency, amount in figures and in words

Выдано рублей
Roubles paid out

Взыскана комиссия
Commission recovered

подпись владельца – holder's signature

(место штампа)

подпись работника банка

Государственный Музей Городской Скульптур

Серия ВК

ВХОДНОЙ БИЛЕТ   15394 ✳

1000

Цена 40

Обязательно сохранить до конца посещения

Настоящая справка выдается исключительно для подтверждения факта обмена иностранной валюты на рубли и права обрат-
ного обмена на иностранную валюту, чеки и или перевода за границу не предоставляет.

This certificate is delivered in confirmation of the fact of exchange of foreign currency for Roubles ONLY and does not
give any right to effect a reexchange for foreign currency, cheques or transfer abroad.

Гос. предпр. тип. № 12, Зак. 910. Тир. 200 000X50X2.

Weston   BANGOR ME.

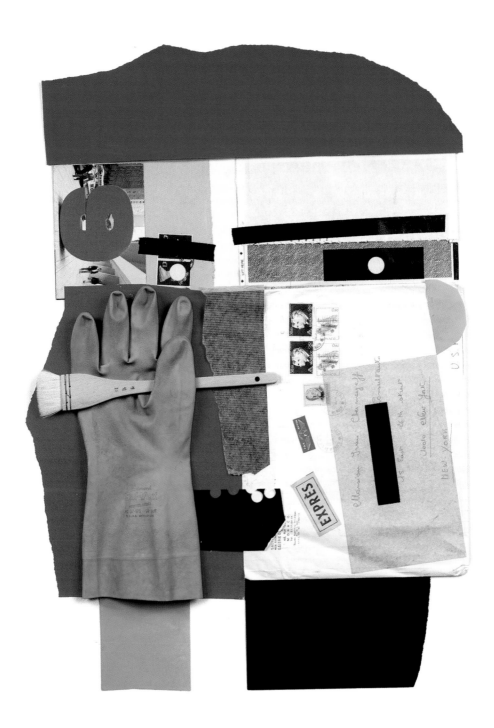

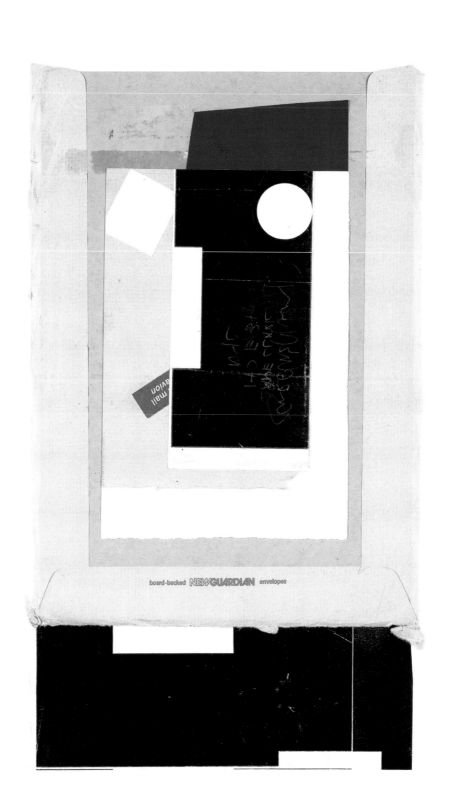

board-backed NEW GUARDIAN envelopes

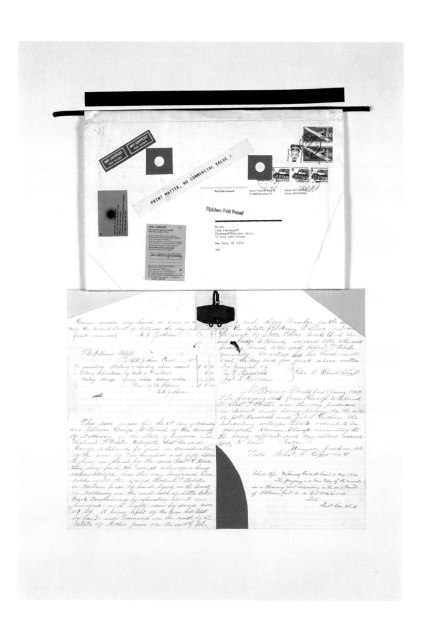

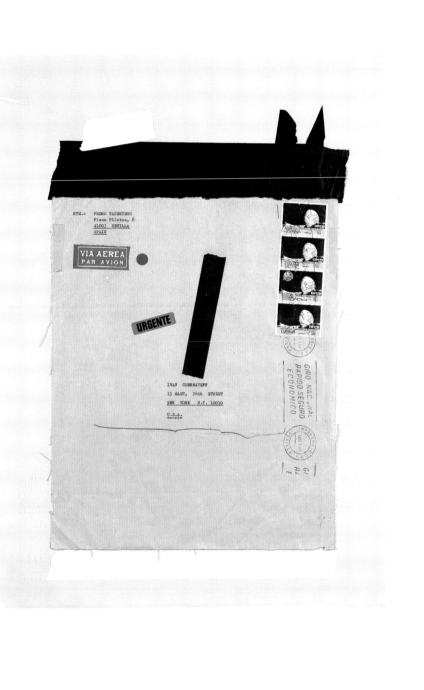

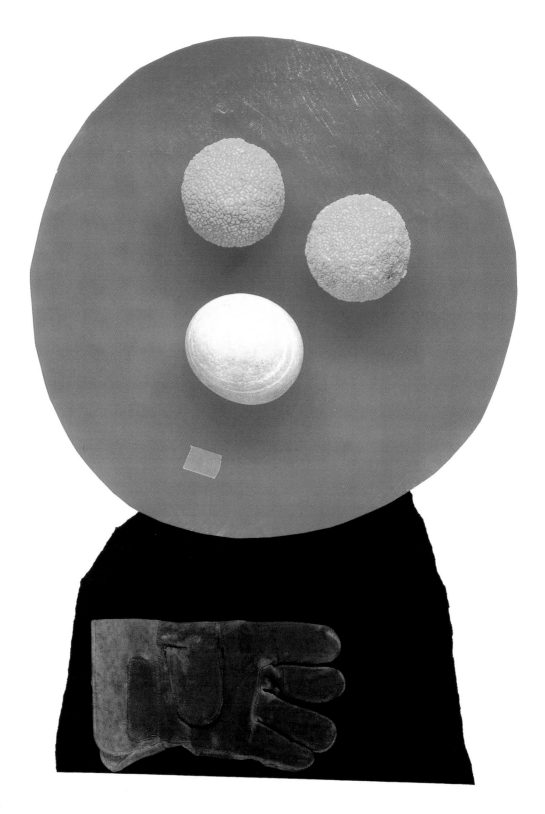

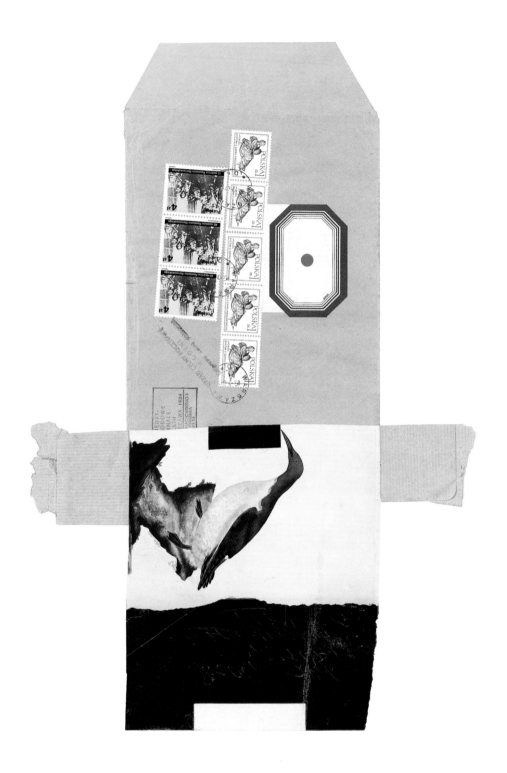

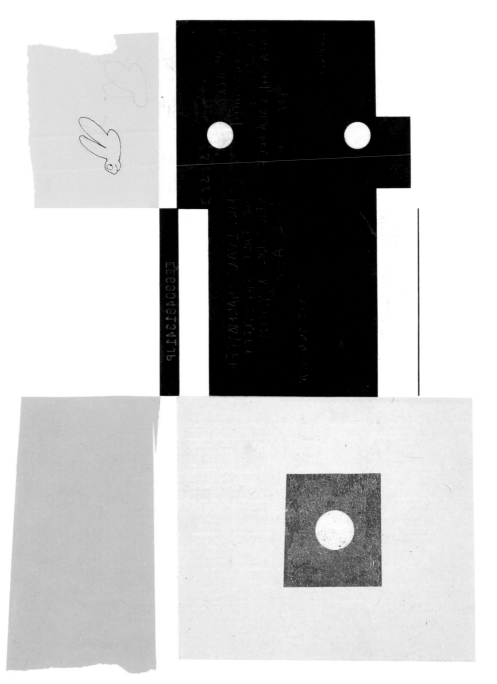

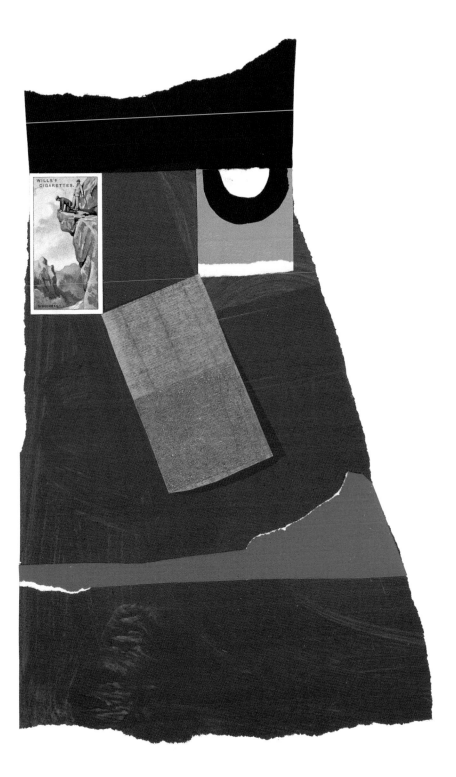

80

82

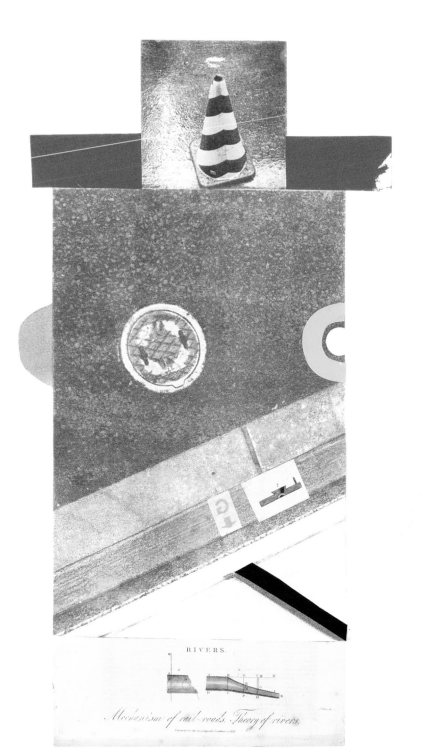

Mr. Ivan Chermayeff
Chermayeff & Geismar
5 East 26th Street
New York, New York 10010

MR IVAN CHERMAYEFF

NEW YORK 10010
USA

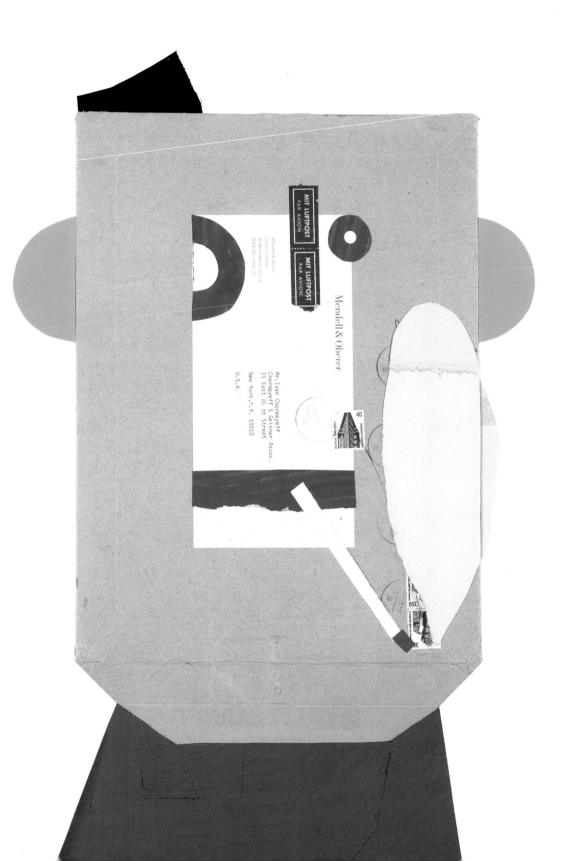

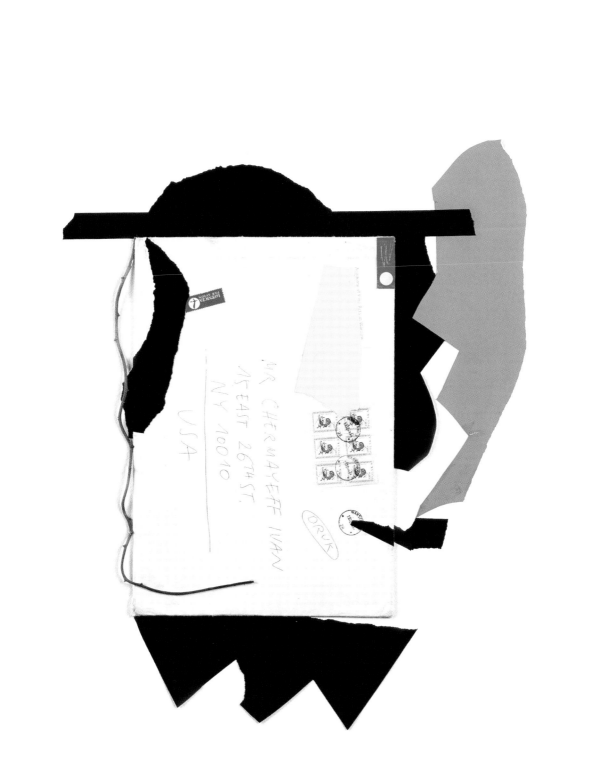

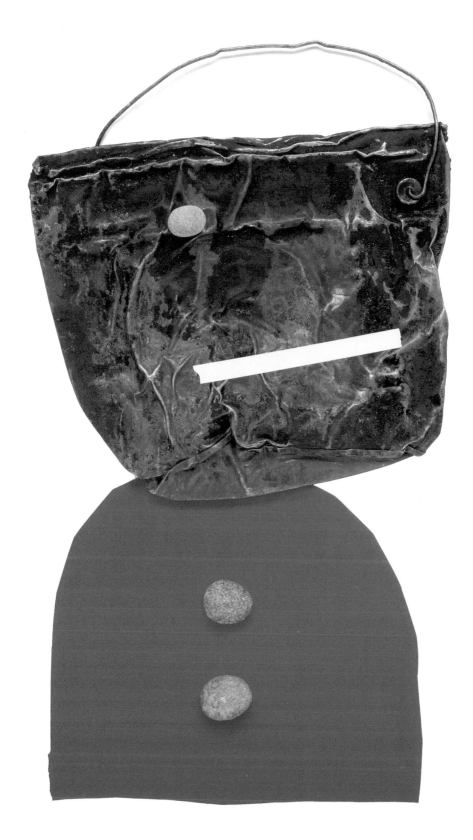

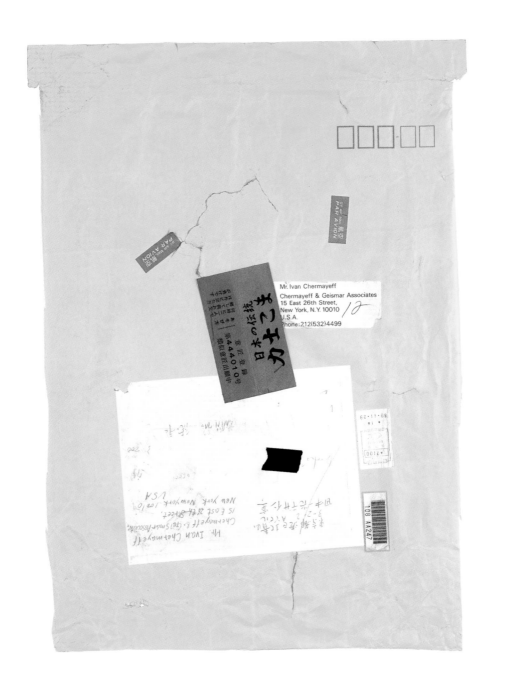

3

The rectifying Still.
&c.

J.Pass sculp!

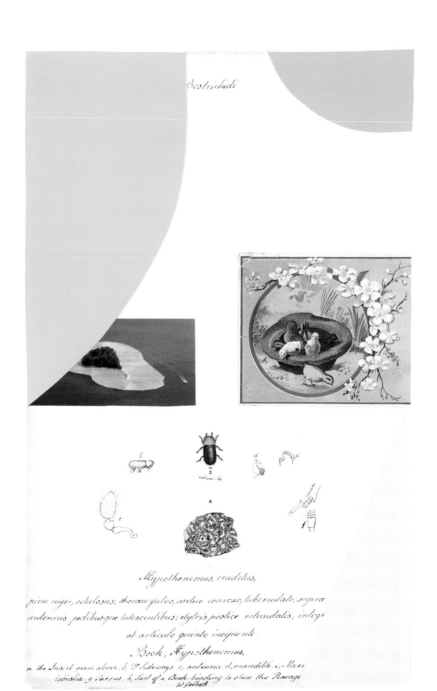

Hypothenemus, crudelis,

piceo niger, setulosus; thorace fulvo, antice convexo, tuberculato, supra antennis pedibusque lutescentibus; elytris postice rotundatis, integr. *ab articulo quinto incipiente.*

Book, Hypothenemus.

a the Insect seen above. b, D. Sideways. c, antenna. d, mandible. e, Maxi labialia. g Tarsus. h, Part of a Book-binding to shew the Ravage

W Goodall

104

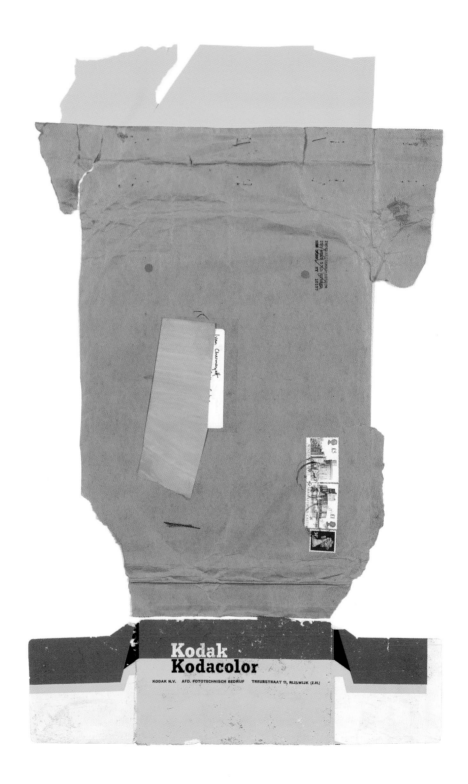

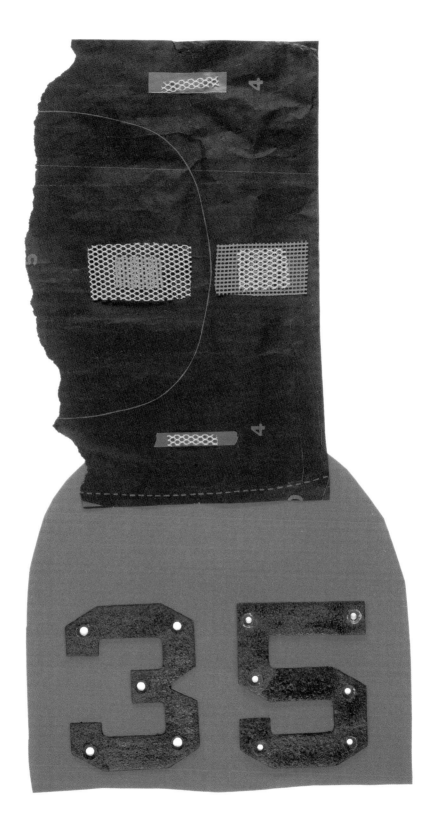

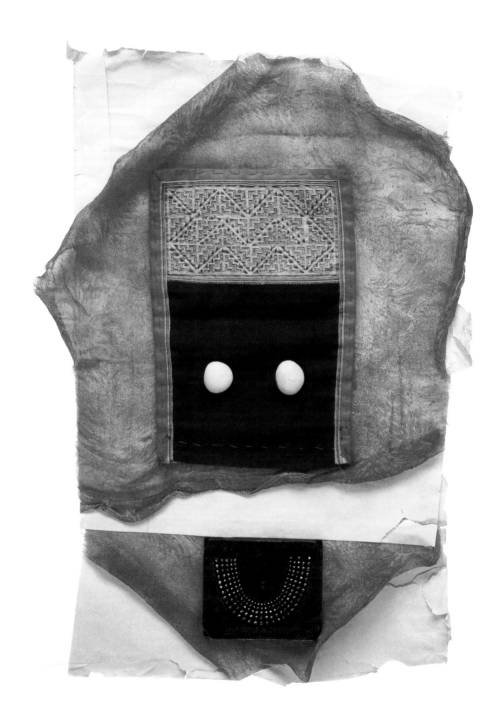

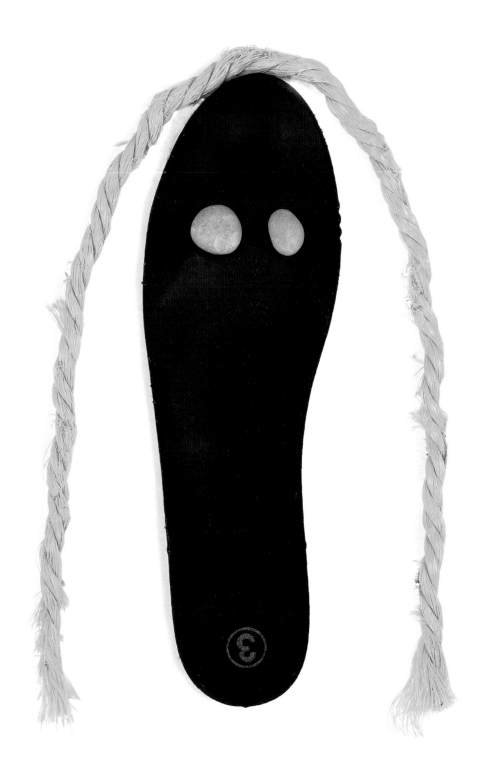

112

Suspects, Soldiers, Smokers and Salesladies
Collages by Ivan Chermayeff

Joseph Giovannini

Trash night in New York has always brought out the city's more
enterprising collagists, but for some twenty-five years, every day has
been bonanza day for Ivan Chermayeff, an eagle-eyed connoisseur
of the city's rich and prolific gutters. "I really like garbage a lot, and
I look at gutters more than streets." The artist has dependably found
gloves in the city's mother-lode, which also regularly offers up ticket
stubs, shoe laces, cigarette packs, candy wrappers. Like a five year old
with a paper sack on an outing to collect leaves, the artist
is fascinated by the textures, colors, and histories of his daily finds,
those *objets trouvés* that he stuffs into his pockets before stowing
in his studio, where the may await their moment for years.

"A good chef goes shopping very carefully, and picks out his own
vegetables, or the fish that just came in—it's very hard to produce
a good meal without good ingredients," he says. "Same thing with
collages. The dish must start with decent beginnings, not just
because of the final taste, but also because of the process of making
it. There are a lot of painters who don't use decent paint. The sur-
faces crack and fade and change colors. There's a certain lack of concern for what you're doing that shows in the work itself."

For Chermayeff, the process of creating a collage is one of a
sequential openness that starts when he crosses the street. He eyes
the gutter with few preconceived notions. But unlike a chef, he is
looking in a place that is usually a repository of cast-offs or leftovers,
and he has become an inveterate packrat with an addiction.
He finds himself peering curiously and hopefully into the pouch
of airline seats, where he can materialize at least a sickness bag, and
he has ventured into drive-in theaters in broad daylight: "One place
was a gold mine—it was like a garden of crushed snow flakes.
The cars drove over the cans of soda. Each one was a unique varia-
tion on a theme."

There is, of course, a long tradition of artists rummaging in unlikely places for materials to include in a painting or sculpture. Picasso famously forged a baboon from a bicycle seat and handlebars, and "painted" with wine labels and stamps. "Picasso had a sensitivity to what was in front of him, and played a game with the relationship between the color and textures and the origins of a piece," says Chermayeff. His collages display the same delight that can be sensed in a Picasso—a mixture of joy, naughtiness, cleverness and improvisation.

Chermayeff's personal history in collage is nearly a half century old, and dates from 1952, after he left Harvard for the Institute of Design/Illinois Institute of Technology in Chicago. "I was probably influenced in a certain way at ID by Aaron Siskind, who was always photographing peeling paint in the landscape," he says. "I liked to make the same kind of discoveries." Chermayeff's early fascination with sandpaper led him to envelopes and the wrappings on cartons later on—that is, to the materials surrounding things. "An old airline ticket is not intended to be an artistic medium—it's just a tool. What interests me is the carbon on its reverse inside."

Chermayeff admits that the early collages came about as a "defense mechanism" against his fear of drawing. "I didn't have the confidence with pencils and brushes but I could draw with scissors," he says. Chermayeff, who went on to become one of America's most talented and celebrated graphic artists, actively resumed his interests in collage a quarter century ago. "I've been doing them more consistently and regularly, and over time, I've become much better at understanding where something can go."

Chermayeff may be a street sweeper's dream pedestrian, but his days are generally routine, like those of most New Yorkers, and there is a biographical cast to the things that find their way into his pockets, as though they were elements of an informal diary. Sometimes he just cleans out his wallet and he finds what any New Yorker would find: ticket stubs, deposit slips, receipts. The economy of objects that circulates through his office enters his collages, and characteristically includes stamps, envelopes, air mail stickers, postcards—all the detritus of his international practice in graphic design. "What's incredible about envelopes is the almost arbitrary placement of labels and stamps that add animation to a piece of paper."

A family man, Chermayeff has shamelessly appropriated the drawings of his son, Sam; he used to talk the boy (now starting college) into standing in dishes of India ink and then walking on paper—all without apology since father fairly compensated son for the high-energy scribblings and footprints with hamburgers and Nintendo monsters. Also pressed into service, the middle of his three daughters, Sasha, painted solid slabs of color on paper in the purest, most saturated blues and greens; blocks of these color painted papers anchor his collages with chromatic depth. When he vacations in Wellfleet, Massachusetts, in the house once owned by his illustrious father, Bauhaus architect and Yale professor Serge Chermayeff, he combs the beach for driftwood and quintessential pebbles. Chermayeff is a maw.

"The wonderful thing about gloves, which you find on a constant basis and never as a pair, is the connection to the human body," he says. "A glove is a hand, unlike a sock, which is not really a foot. A glove does my job in a collage. I keep picking up gloves on the street where construction workers loose them. So I'm always looking around at this stuff which is discarded—the gum wrappers and cigarette packages that are left over and flattened out by civilization marching over them. All of these things happen to be out there, and I get a hold of them. The part of the Polaroid that you don't use is more interesting than the photo itself. I carry a great big case of all my collections of stuff."

The discoveries tend to fall into categories, each with its own material character. "Gloves have a wonderful quality, especially when they're made of leather. Carbon has a density, whether black or red, which is truly intense, and it has these strange indentations which mean nothing. When you use it, you get the history in reverse. With pebbles, every one is different, but they all contain within them pebbleness. Pebbles become eyes, mouths and buttons. Gloves remain hands."

He trawls everywhere—on the streets, in his office, in the apartment—and "shops" over a period of weeks for the ingredients until the accumulation reaches critical mass. "I need to allow things to stew and ferment, and in a burst of activity that may last a full week straight, I produce a lot of work." Chermayeff pieces together the collages by a process of associative thinking. He is not so much interested in the tradition of collage, but lives in intense moments of free association. A scrap may suggest a face or figure, and then one thing reminds him of something else in a pile. Sometimes a piece is sitting right in front of him, within arm's reach, but other times he finds it by radar, with near-total recall of his inventory. There's a flash of recognition as he makes a spontaneous connection between like or unlike things. "The more quickly and less inhibited, the better," he says. "I like things that come without too much laboring. It's very easy to overcook things."

Wit has been defined as the unexpected copulation of disparate ideas, and the accidental and serendipitous matings of things that Chermayeff brings together breed visual repartee. Something new and rich occurs when materials with different graphic or tactile qualities collide in his compositions. "I love the idea of discovering that two things that have no relationship are the same size and color," he says. "It's like a chef who discovers that bananas are perfectly OK with fish—there are new relationships that when made, come to life."

"The whole thing is an intense search for connections among the ingredients, even if they're unsophisticated. I can get quite excited by a piece of paper torn out of political posters from thirty years ago. They may not be good posters, but the letters could be interesting, and when I cut them up, an endless series of observations arises, and I begin to see other worlds. There's a difference between cut and torn and brushed edges. I can get excited by putting up one black against a carbon black and finding out that black is not really black. You're distracted by form, but then you add some wonderful material from another time, like an image from an old encyclopedia, and papers that have disappeared from our lives—old bills, indentures, from the turn of the century." The occasional piece of writing becomes a texture in this context; handwriting itself—the extraordinary penmanship of ordinary clerks—becomes an object. "It doesn't matter what the piece of paper says; the quality of a hand at work just emerges (penmanship has been downhill for a long time). My collages often take advantage of what someone else has done, though I use the pieces without any relationship to content."

Often a simple detail locks the whole composition into place. "It doesn't take much to turn an envelope into a face, perhaps just a white dot that makes a mouth. By adding a mouth, you establish some rules because there's a relationship with the rest of the features—the eyes, nose, ears. When you have a head, a glove might give you the hand, and it might be waving hello. A little touch of tape might suggest a hat, but something messier, with fuzzy edges might make the portrait look like Carmen Miranda." Smoking intrigues him and appears as a leitmotif, "an edgeless thing, a non-form form" rising from a face.

There is a magic quality in the discarded objects that Chermayeff transfigures into a work of art, in the wisp of plastic grass from a sushi dish that he uses as a crop of green hair. But there is also transportational quality to collages that have powers of a magic carpet or a time machine. However humble, each piece has a provenance that is usually recognizable, and the sense of another place or time within these neatly framed collages tenses the abstract composition with associations outside the frame. The slip of paper might have come from Germany or Japan, or from Sam's classroom, but they imply other orbits outside the dense world Chermayeff creates.

One of artist's recurring genres is the portrait, and though he has an unerring eye for composition, he is also a visual sociologist and psychologist who builds character in his constructions. Though he doesn't start to make a specific character, "when you deal with eyes, nose, mouth, then character, and personality emerge," he says. "I push it." With an incredible economy of means, sometimes entailing no more than a few loops of string, he invents people—it might be a stolid matriarch, the kind of woman that smokes, maybe even cigars, or a simple-minded guide whose only flamboyance resides in a thunderous cap. "I do think about these personalities with a certain amount of comic realization," he says. "It's funny to see a character emerge."

The same can be said of the character of his collages: the work embodies a temperament. These portraits, as art, possess a lightness of spirit that is no less intelligent for being charming. The imagery may play in the intriguing visual ambiguity between abstraction and representation, but it also takes the viewer into its confidence, as though sharing a humorous secret. The invitation to the secret lies in the incompletion. With a tremendous economy of means at the service of an infallible eye, Chermayeff never makes his images explicit, but leaves them suggestively fragmented. One pebble may not be matched by another; a sharp edge may correspond to a fuzzy edge. His open forms and wide references take us into his process by asking our eye and mind to make synaptic leaps, to complete the portraits in our own perception.

These are elliptical works that, like puzzles, challenge us to make the connections that Chermayeff has made, to bring the fragments into a whole. The wisdom of his wit is that his invention beckons us into our own invention. We are the participants in its creation.

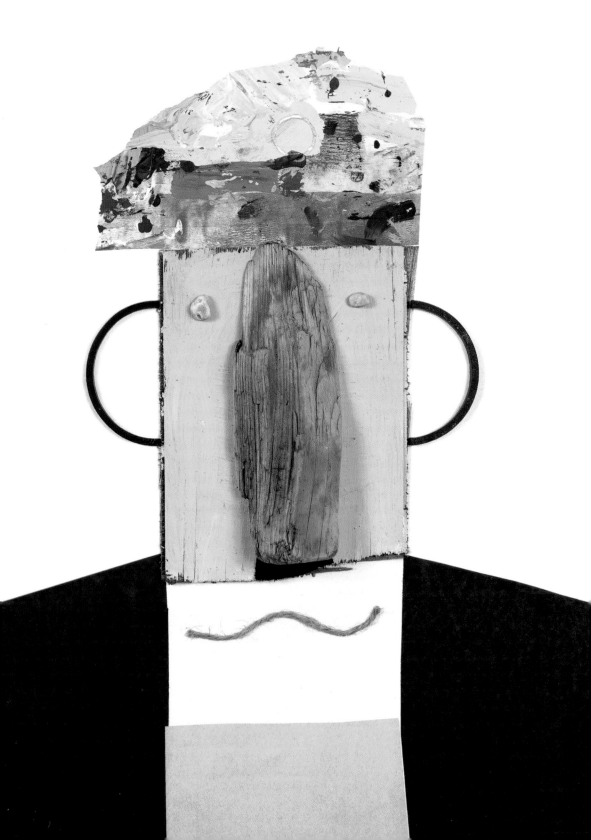

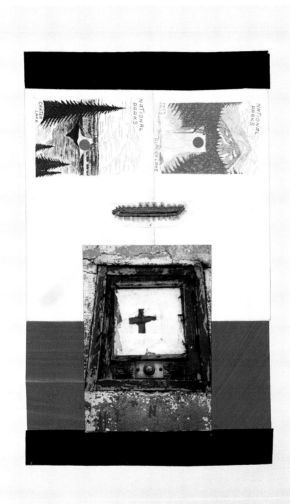

126

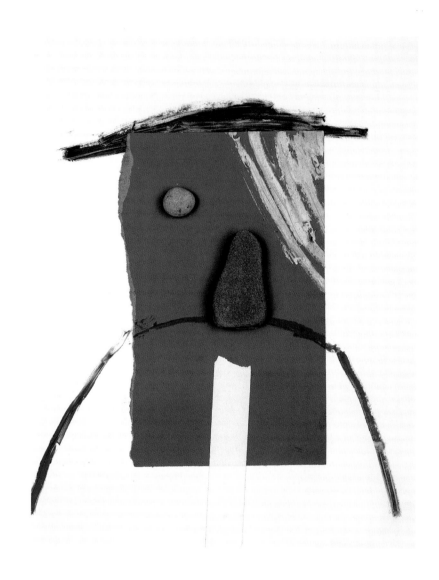

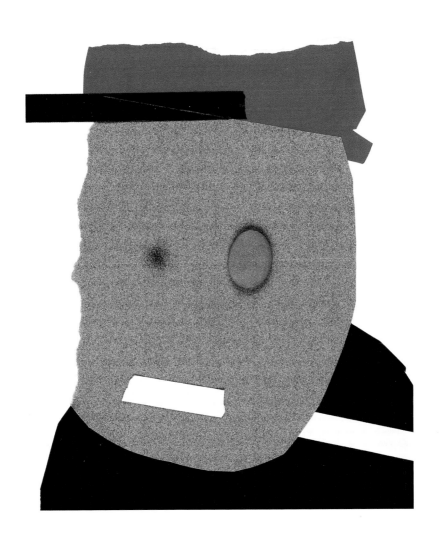

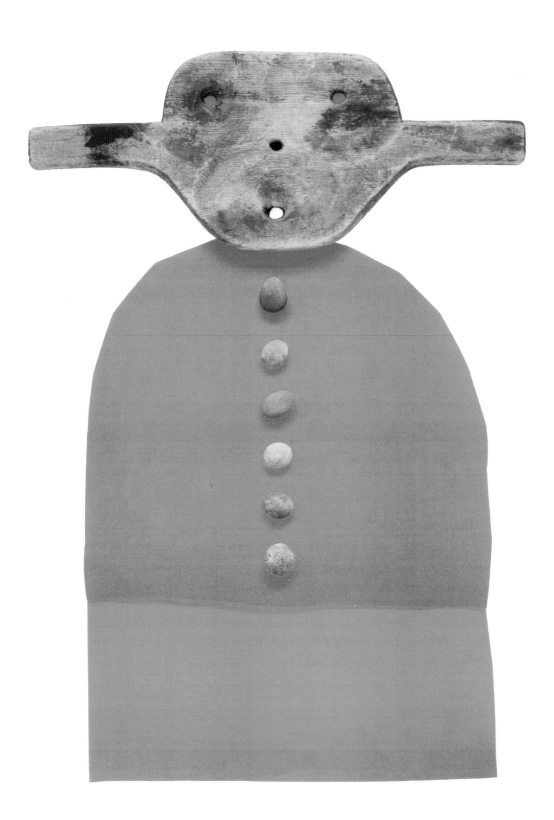

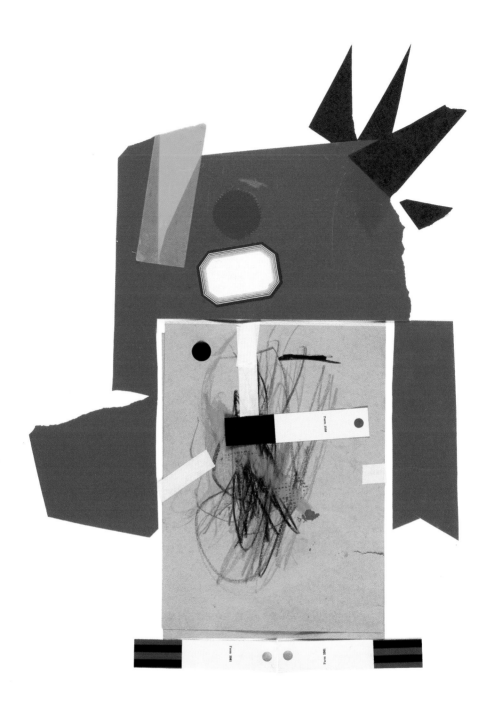

LIFT HERE

Mr. Ivan Chermayeff

香港 20
HONG KONG

香港 20
HONG KONG

香港 5

U.S.A.
New York, N.Y. 10010
12 East 32nd Street.
Chermayeff & Geismar Inc.
Mr. Ivan Chermayeff

JAPAN

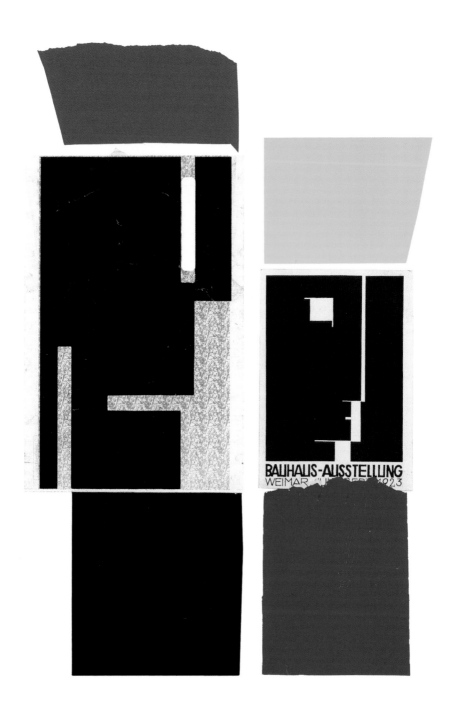

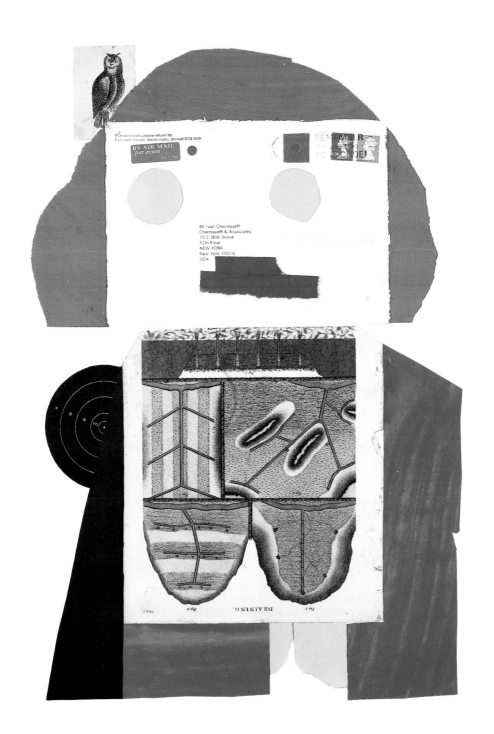

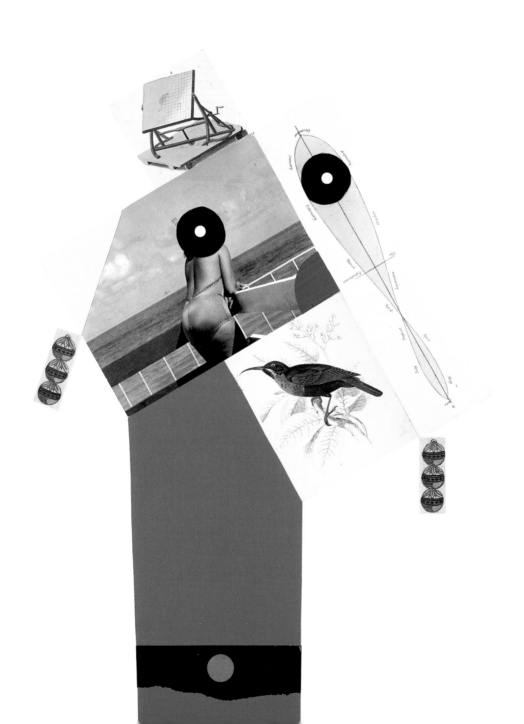

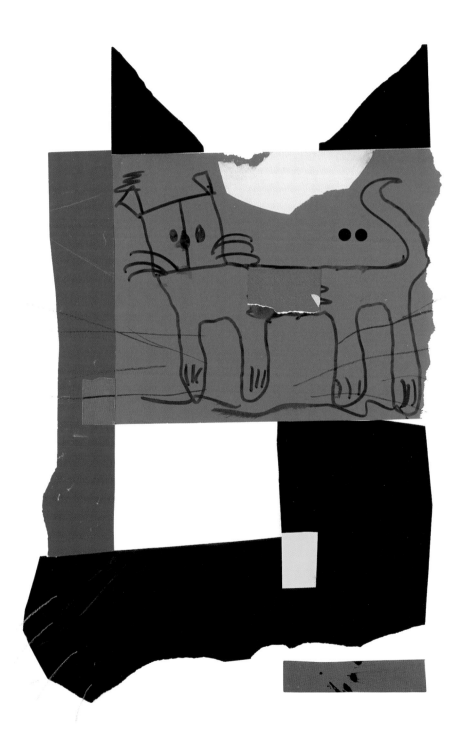

163 S...
23. VI...

新宿

163 SHINJU
23. VI. 92

M. Chermayeff Ivan

AIR MAIL

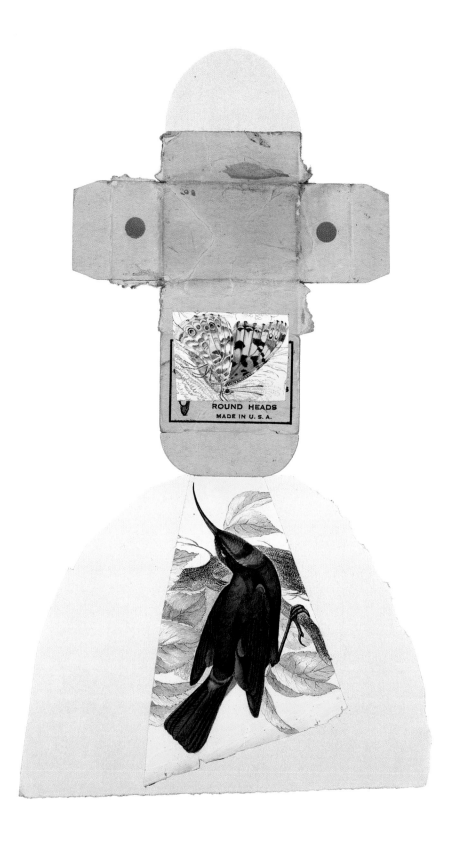

ROUND HEADS
MADE IN U.S.A.

Insecta,
Coleoptera,
Buprestidæ.

Buprestis Salicis, Fab. Illiger.

Elytris integerrimis, viridis, nitens, coleopteris aureis, basu viridebus.

Willow Buprestis

(B. Gmelin.)

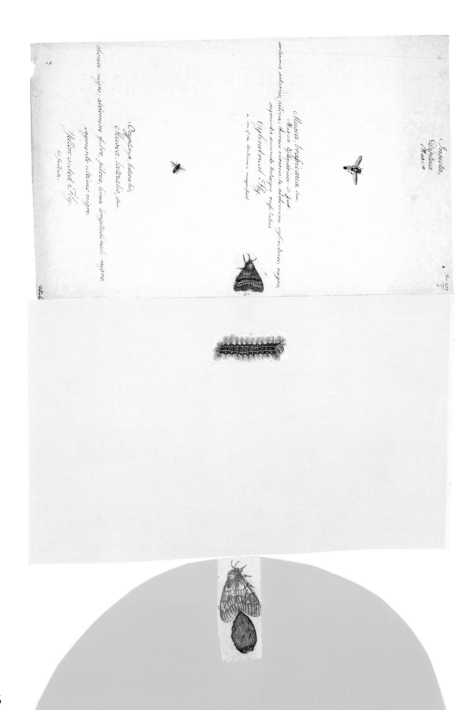

166

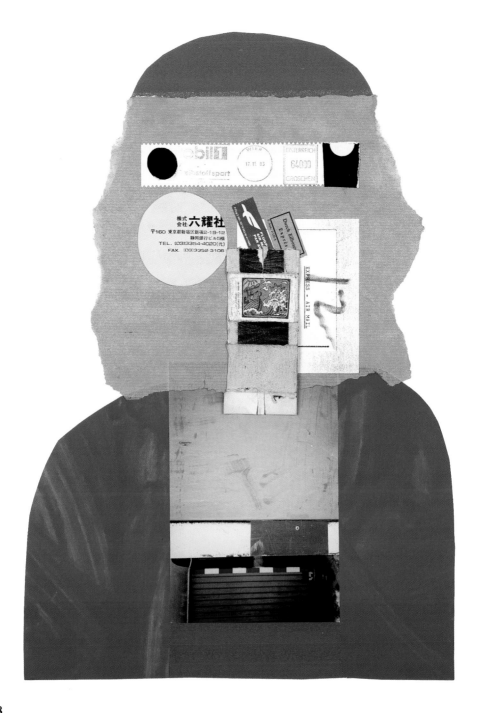

168

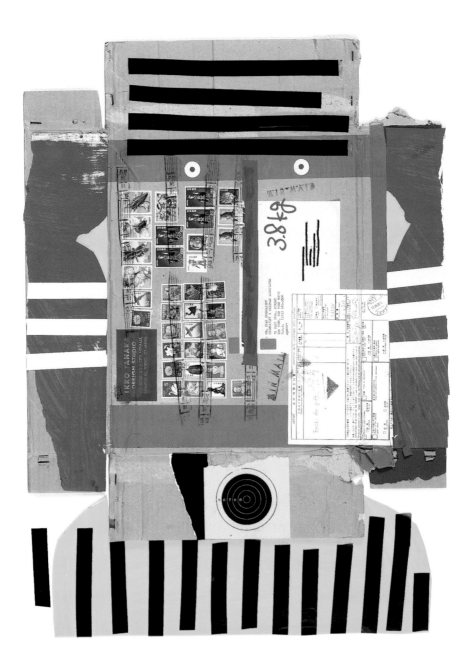

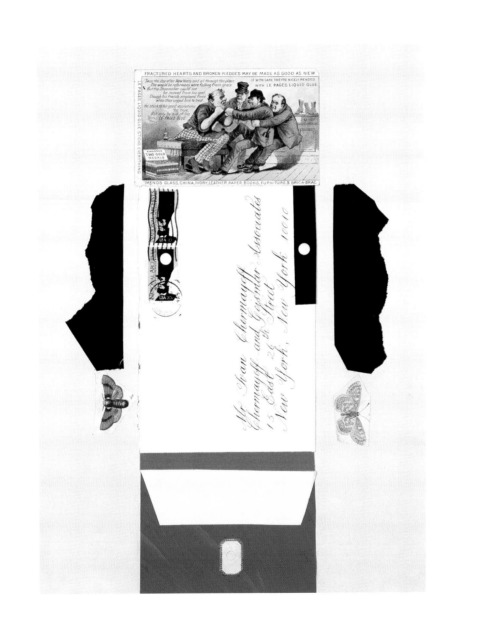

172

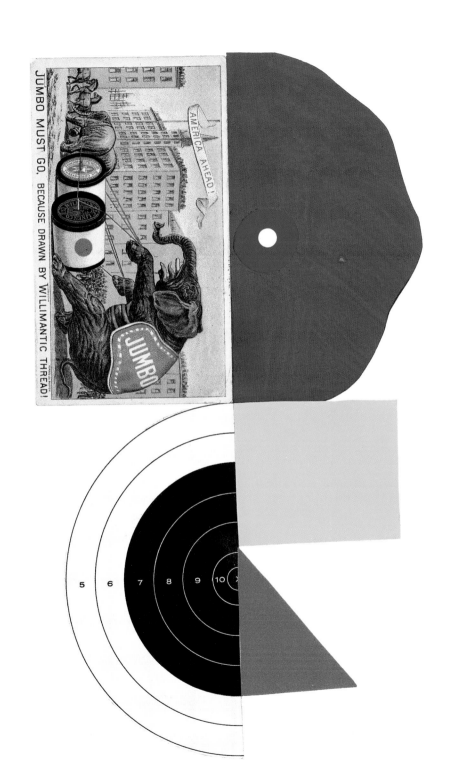

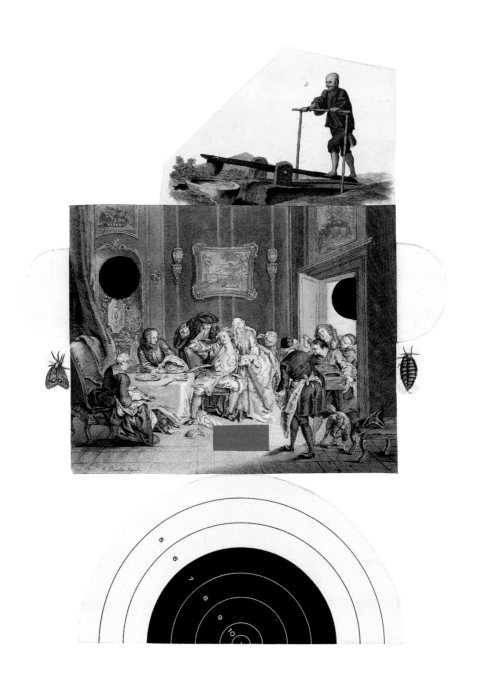

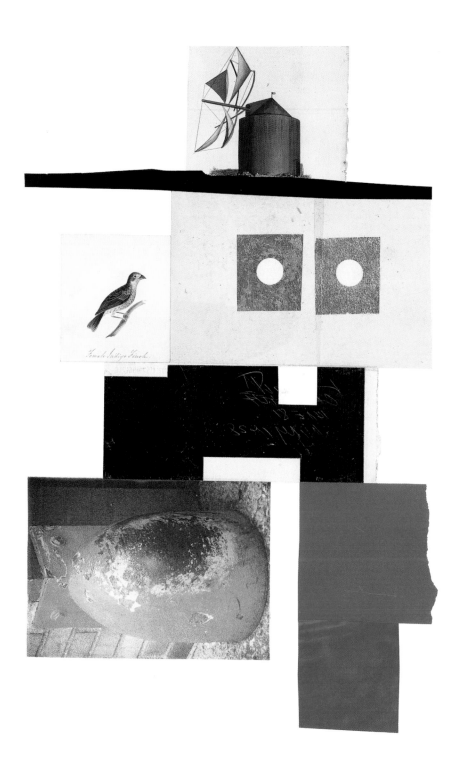

The President and Mrs. Clinton
request the pleasure of your company
at an awards ceremony to be held at
The White House
on Monday morning, September 29, 1997
at eight o'clock

TD

Associatie voor Total Design bv
Postbus 19805
1000 GV Amsterdam

• Chermayeff + Geismar Ass. Inc.
Attn. Mr. Ivan Chermayeff
15 East 26th Street
New York, N.Y. 10010
USA

LUCHTPOST
PAR AVION

NEDERLAND 60 CENT

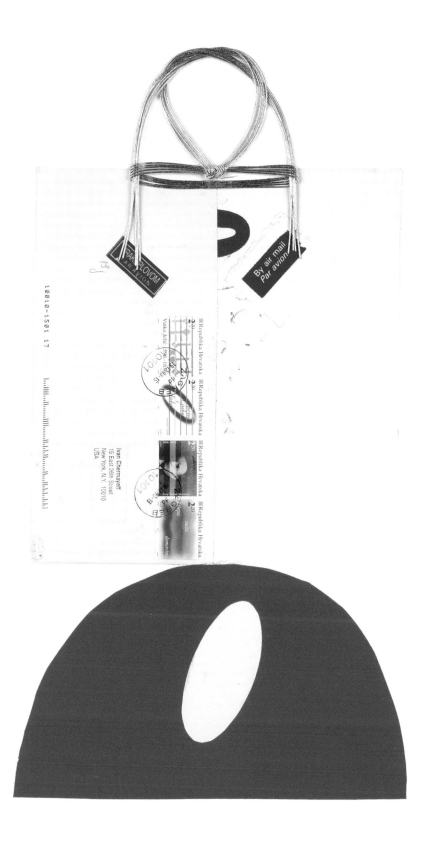

By air mail
Par avion

Ivan Chermayeff
Chermayeff & Geismar Inc
15 East 26th Street
12th Floor
New York NY 10010
United States of America

USA · USA
CHERNAYEFF IVAN
15 EAST 26th St.
NEW YORK, NY 10010
UNITED STATES

Par avion

189600 LENiNGRAD
KoLPiNO-5
St. OKTABRSKAIA
h.55, 9.45
ALEXANDR FALDiN

The President and Mrs. Clinton
request the pleasure of your company
at an awards ceremony to be held at
The White House
on Monday morning September 22 1997
at eight o'clock

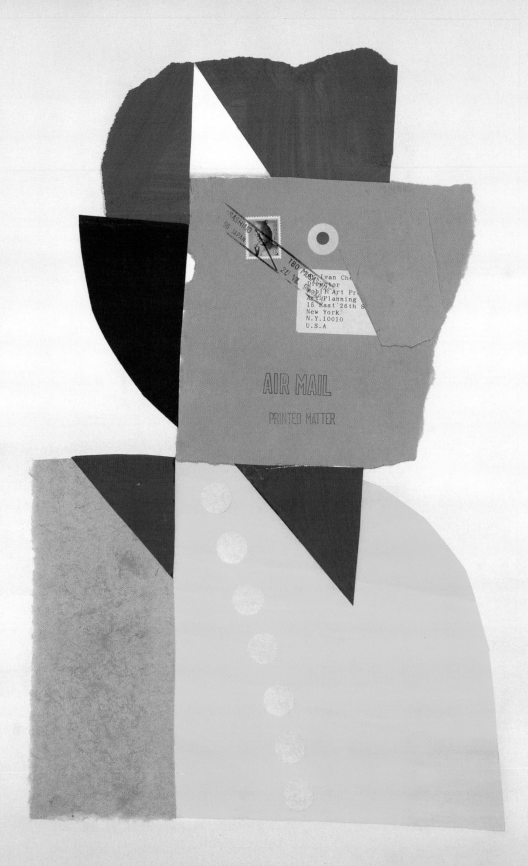

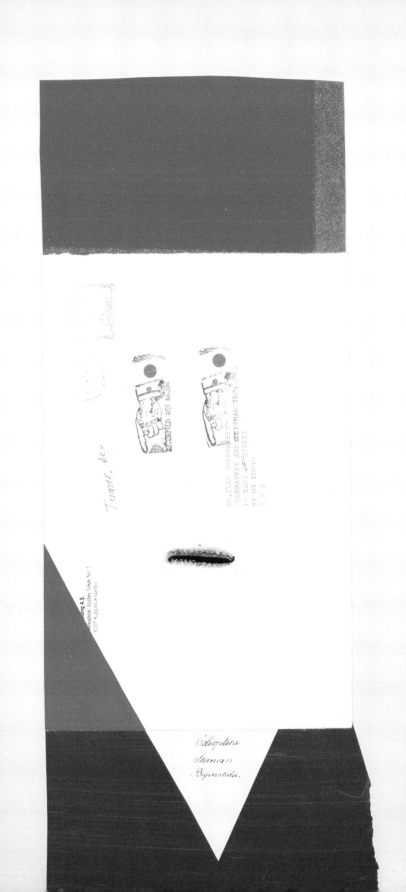

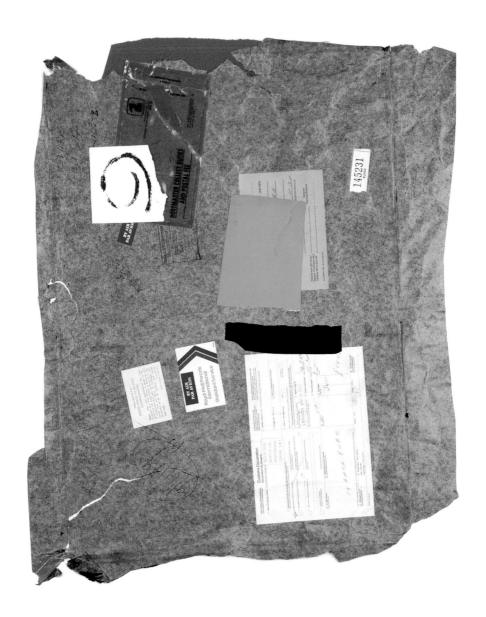

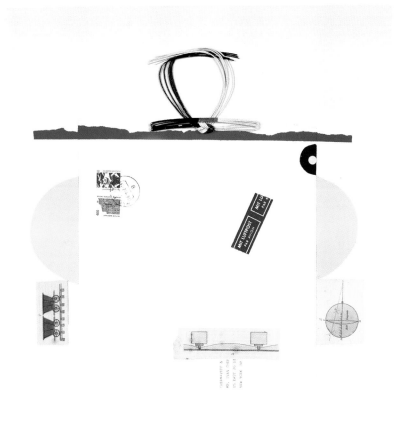

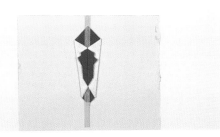

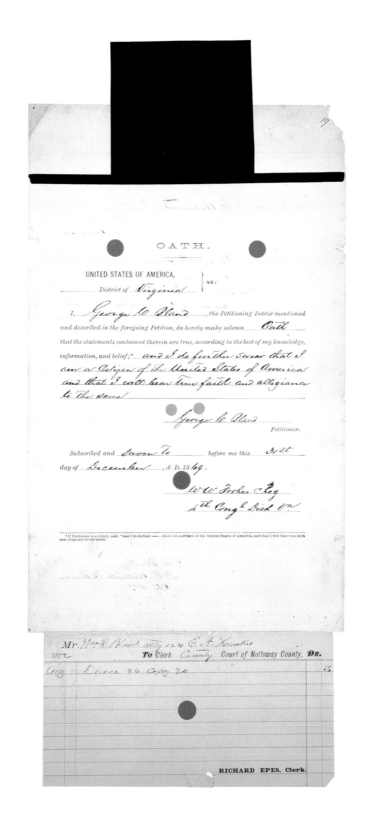

OATH.

UNITED STATES OF AMERICA,
District of *Virginia* } *ss:*

I, *George C Bland*, the Petitioning Debtor mentioned and described in the foregoing Petition, do hereby make solemn *Oath* that the statements contained therein are true, according to the best of my knowledge, information, and belief;* *and I do further swear that I am a Citizen of the United States of America and that I will bear true faith and allegiance to the same*

George C Bland

Petitioner.

Subscribed and *sworn to* before me this *31st* day of *December*, A. D. 18 *69*.

W W Forbes Esq
4th Congl Dist Va

*If Petitioner is a citizen, add: "and I do further ——— that I am a citizen of the United States of America, and that I will bear true faith and allegiance to the same."

Mr Wm R Bland atty in E A Hawkins
18*72*   **To** Clerk *County* Court of Nottoway County. **Dr.**

Aug Decree 36 Copy 20   *56*

RICHARD EPES, Clerk.

19   Grand Central Terminal, New York City

3A-H1287

Mr. and Mrs. Ivan Chermayeff

Sheep's Hill

North Salem, New York

10560

30th ANNIVERSARY
Launch of Bumper No. 8
First Missile
Launched at Cape Canaveral
July 24, 1950, Kennedy Space Center

KENNEDY SPACE CENTER
JUL
24
1980
32815 FL

Einstein
USA 15c

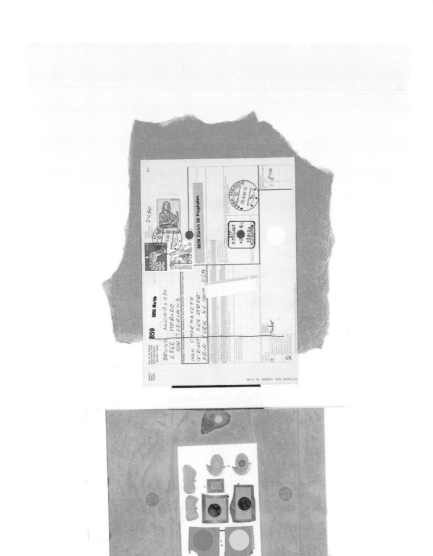

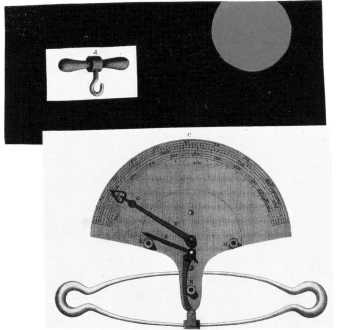

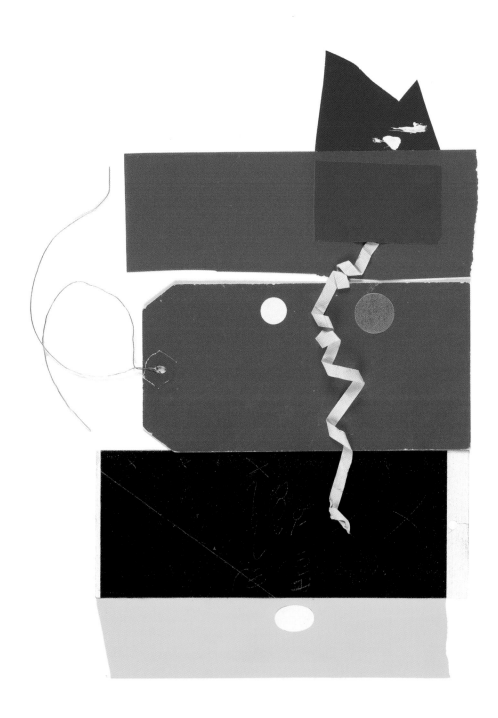

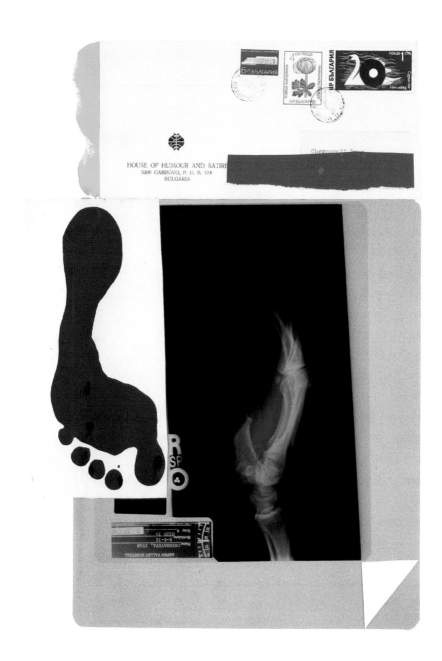

HOUSE OF HUMOUR AND SATIRE
5300 GABROVO, P. O. B. 104
BULGARIA

218

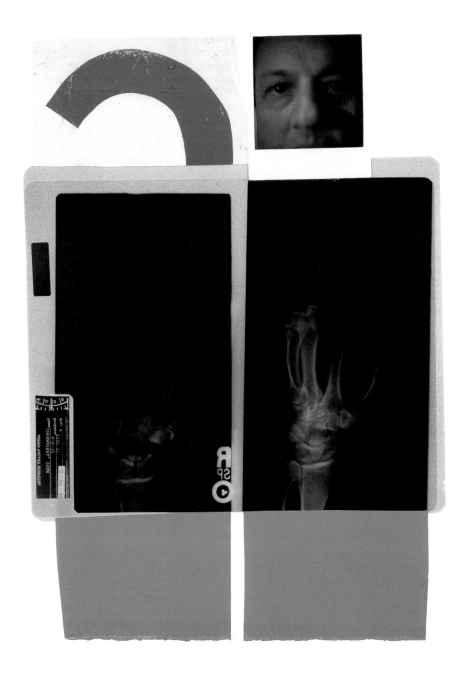

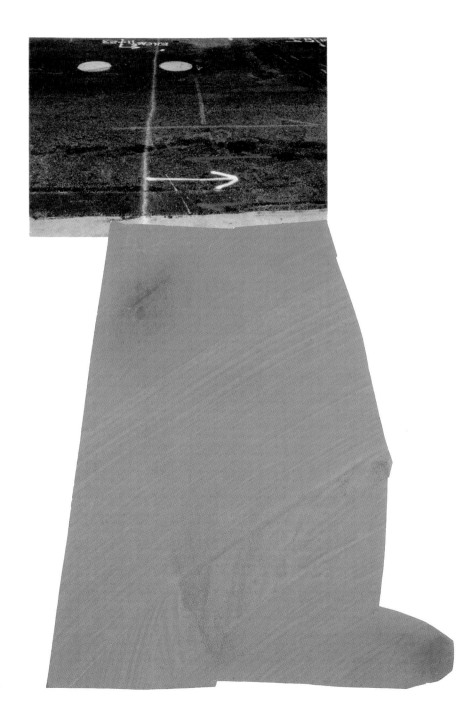

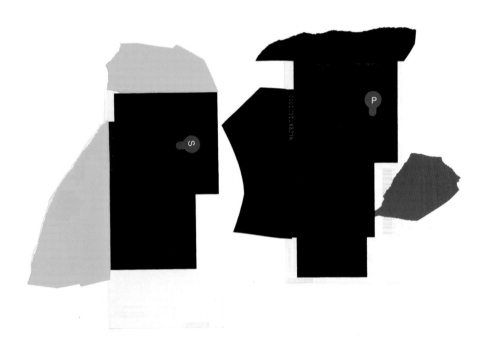

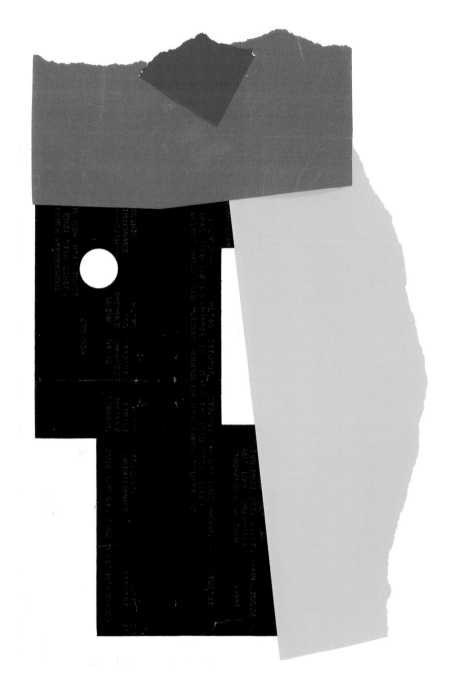

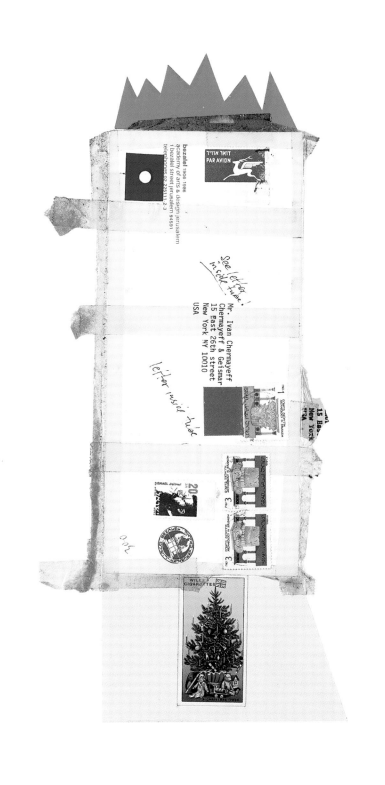

bezalel 1906·1986
academy of arts & design jerusalem
1 bezalel street jerusalem 94591
telephones 02·225111.2·3

דואר אויר
PAR AVION

See letter
inside tube!

Mr. Ivan Chermayeff
Chermayeff & Geismar
15 East 26th street
New York NY 10010
USA

letter inside tube

ISRAEL

15 East
New York
USA

ISRAEL

20

WILLS
CIGARETTES

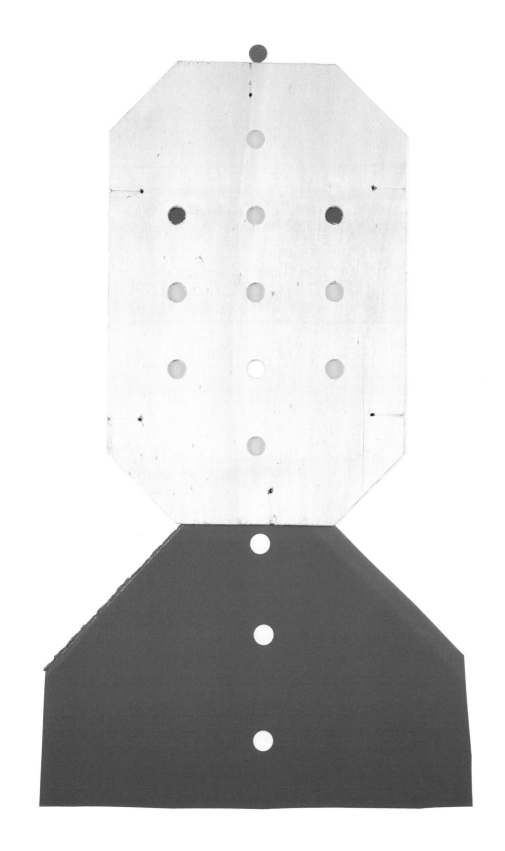

Chambre N° 16   Fol: 592

HÔTEL BAUR en VILLE.   HÔTEL et PENSION BAUR au LAC.

F. ZIESING-BAUR, ZURICH.

NOTE pour Mon Moeu

Le service du portier de l'étage n'est pas compris.

Lith. F. Fretz Zürich.

1872				Frcs.	Cts.
Dbre	7	2 Thés Compl	3		
		2 Compotes	1.50	4	50
		Bougie & chauffage		2	
	8	2 Déjeuners	3.—		
		2 Dîners	7.—		
		2 Thés Compl	3.—	15	50
		1½ Chapon	2.50		
	9	2 Dejr.	3		
		2 Beefs & pommes	4	7	—
		3 Dîners		10	50
		Logement		10	—
		Service		4	
		fr		53	50

Pr acquit
po Ziesing
Selmer

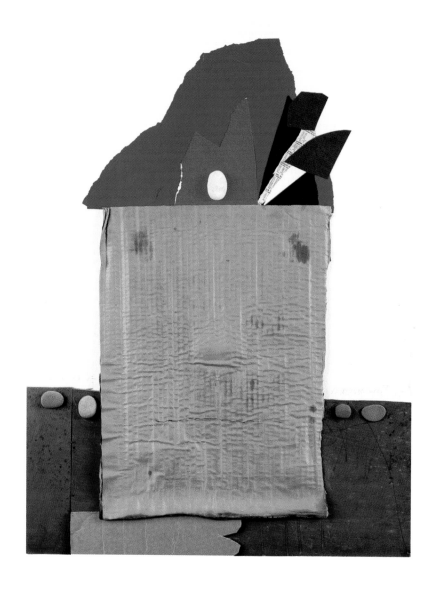

234

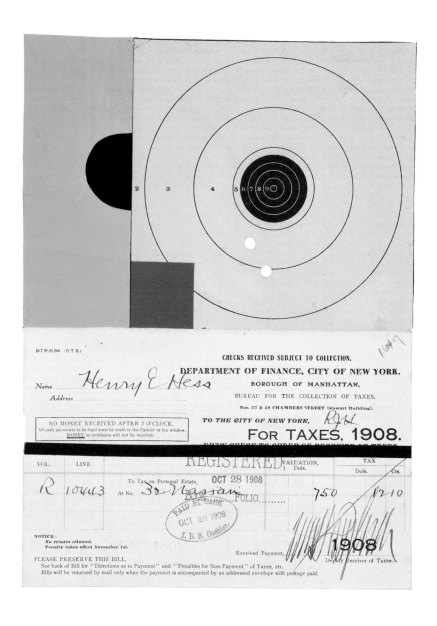

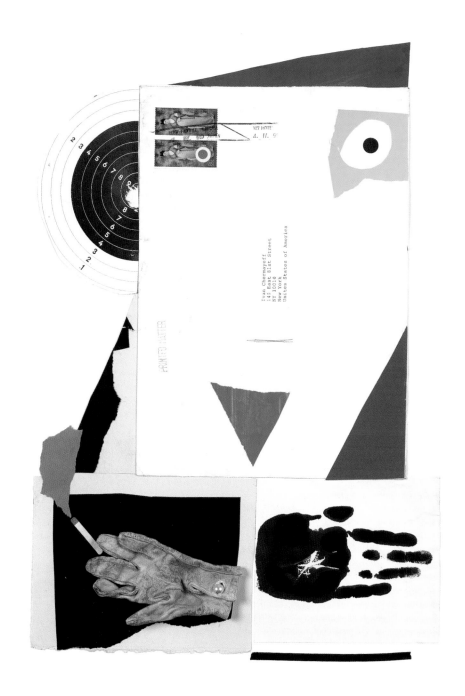

246

248

1	Type Face II	22 x 15"	2000
2	Lincoln	22 x 15"	1993
	Collection: Guy Barron		
3	Chrysomela	22 x 15"	1990
4	Type Face VII	22 x 15"	2000
5	Phil Hawks	22 x 15"	2000
6	Big Mouth	15 x 11"	1998
7	Girl	14 1/2 x 11 1/2"	2000
8	Man Leaving	14 x 11"	1996
17	Grinning Fool with Chris Irving's Cat	30 x 22"	1994
	Collection: Watson Powell		
18	Spaniard with Polish Eye	15 x 11"	2000
19	Female Bird of Prey	22 x 15"	1990
	Collection: John Sailer		
20	A with Hummingbird	30 x 22"	2000
21	Spaniard	15 x 11"	1998
22	Foot Arm	22 x 15"	2000
23	Israeli Soldier Smiling	30 x 22"	1995
24	D-Day Veteran	30 x 22"	1994
	Collection: George Kravis		
25	Vet	19 x 15"	1998
26	Fire Worker	15 x 11"	2000
27	Sphinx	21 x 24"	2000
28	German Ship's Captain	22 x 15"	2000
29	Eiko	15 x 11"	1998
30	Slovakian Graphiste	30 x 22 1/2"	1997
31	Burri and Porter	18 x 13"	1999
	Collection: Jane Clark Chermayeff		
32	Blue Beret	15 x 11"	1998
	Collection: Sarah L. Kearns		
33	Austrian Swiss Border Guard	22 x 16"	1994
34	Hero	19 x 14"	1994
35	Border Guard	30 x 22"	1995
36	Pole	15 x 11"	1998
37	Israeli Falconer with Tomato	30 x 22"	1998
38	Official Bore	22 x 15"	1995
	Collection: Private		
39	Little English Girl	22 x 15"	1990
40	Dubuffet Mouth	15 x 11"	1998
41	Doorman at the Lindenhof	22 x 15"	1998
42	Brown Nose	22 x 15"	2000
43	Young Man	15 x 11"	2000

44	Israeli Syrian	15 x 11"	2000
45	Ricky Alfierez	30 x 22"	2000
46	Russian Boy	18 x 13"	1999
47	Sam	14 x 11 1/2"	1994
	Collection: Sam Clark Chermayeff		
48	Lady with Butterfly Earrings	30 x 22 1/2"	1997
49	Woman with Hat	22 1/2 x 15"	1996
50	T Mouth	22 x 15"	2000
51	Johnson	19 x 15"	1997
52	String Tie	30 x 22"	2000
53	Danish Poster Person	22 x 15"	2000
54	Touraco	15 x 11"	1998
	Collection: Craig O'Brien		
55	Type Face XI	15 x 11"	2000
56	Earl of Plymouth	15 x 11"	1998
57	Balinese Princess	30 x 22"	1993
58	Seal Eyes	18 x 12"	1995
	Collection: Sasha Chermayeff		
59	Folk Artist	15 x 11"	1998
60	Road Killer	30 x 22"	1992
61	Target	47 x 35"	1999
	Iris Print		
62	Monkey	29 1/2 x 21"	1994
	Collection: Watson Powell		
63	Harlequin	30 x 24"	1991
	Collection: Dai Nippon		
64	Tree Nose	19 x 15"	1997
65	Bird Man	15 x 11"	1998
	Collection: Craig O'Brien		
66	Ruble Exchanger	15 x 13"	1999
67	Sarah Campbell	15 x 11"	2000
68	Man with Grey Sleeve	25 x 15"	2000
	Collection: Jack Summerford		
69	Man with an Anastasi Hand	22 x 15"	2000
70	Painter from Monaco	29 1/2 x 21"	1994
	Collection: Sherry Nevins		
71	New Guardian	22 x 15"	1987
72	Deed for Uwe Loesch	30 x 21"	1999
73	Spaniard with Eye Patch	19 x 13 1/2"	1990
74	Fruit Eyes	47 x 35"	1999
	Iris Print		
75	Short Priest	19 x 15"	1997
76	Polish Doll with Bird Beard	22 1/2 x 15"	1997
77	Whistler	15 x 11"	1995

78	Little Clown	15 x 11"	2000
79	Gold Diggers	15 x 11"	1998
80	Hong Kong Dealer	18 x 12"	1995
81	Young Smoker	22 x 18"	1992
82	Constructivist Smoker	18 x 12"	1995
83	Railroad Smoker	22 1/2 x 15"	1997
84	Worker	14 x 11"	1996
85	Richard	15 x 11"	1998
86	Batman Smoking	30 x 22"	1993
	Collection: Guy Barron		
87	Pierre	22 x 15"	1998
88	Road Face	15 x 11 1/2"	1997
	Collection: Gus & Liz Oliver		
89	Sephardic Smoker	30 x 22"	1990
90	Small Face	22 x 19"	1987
91	Norwegian Smoker	22 x 15"	1998
92	Smoker	28 x 22"	1991
	Silkscreen Print		
93	Algerian Pirate	22 1/2 x 15"	1995
94	Urchin	35 x 23"	1999
	Iris Print		
95	Innocent Japanese Person	29 x 22"	1991
	Silkscreen Print		
96	Fagin	30 x 22"	1986
	Collection: Private		
97	Grace	15 x 11"	2000
98	Barrel Mouth	15 x 11"	2000
99	Sky Eye	15 x 11"	2000
100	Dog Face	22 x 21"	1995
101	Christo Island Lady	15 x 11"	2000
102	Butterfly Man	30 x 22 1/2"	1997
103	African with Brian's Note	30 x 22"	1990
104	Monkey Face from Uwe Loesch	30 x 22"	1992
105	Target Head	30 x 22"	1999
106	Photo Technician	30 x 22 1/2"	1993
107	Nazca	35 x 23"	1999
	Iris Print		
108	Sleeve	23 1/2 x 17 1/2"	1999
	Iris Print		
109	Head	12 1/2 x 10"	1996
110	Beach Bum	22 x 17"	1997
111	Thief	17 x 14"	1996
112	Guy with Sam's Hand	30 x 22"	1999

121	Korean	22 x 15"	1997
	Collection: Gyo & Courtney Obata		
122	Old Artist	22 1/2 x 17 1/2"	1997
123	Old Beach Comber	22 x 17 1/2"	1998
124	Madam	15 x 11"	1998
125	Park Ranger	15 x 11"	1998
126	Runner	18 1/2" x 14"	1998
127	Munch Lady Running	14 x 11"	1993
	Collection: Jane Clark Chermayeff		
128	Prospector	14 x 11"	1993
129	One-eyed Delivery Man	15 x 11"	1992
	Collection: Marshall Erdman and		
	Associates		
130	Child	19 x 12 1/2"	1999
131	Tibetan Monk	35 x 23"	1999
	Iris Print		
132	Chinese Soldier	30 x 22"	1986
	Collection: Jonathan & Diana Rose		
133	Russian Dog	18 x 13"	1999
	Iris Print		
134	Priest	14 x 11"	1993
135	Bearded Boatman	22 x 15"	1999
136	Quail Hat	22 x 15"	1999
137	Colorado Boatman	21 x 15"	1999
	Collection: Peter & Andrea		
	Chermayeff		
138	Red Face	15 x 11"	1998
139	Young Man with Red Hat	15 x 11"	1998
140	Theo Van Doesburg	22 x 15"	1989
	Collection: Rudolph deHarak		
141	Nauseous One	14 x 11"	1996
142	Carbon Mask with Cap	15 x 11"	1987
	Collection: Private		
143	Constructavist Mask I	15 x 11"	1982
144	Ken	14 1/2 x 11 1/2"	1996
145	Black Lady	14 x 11"	1996
	Collection: George Stevens		
146	Black Jockey	19 x 14"	1995
	Collection: Guy Barron		
147	Hong Kong Doorman	15 x 11"	1998
148	Kabuki Tanaka	22 1/2" x 15"	1990
149	Staring Man	14 x 11"	1996
150	Bauhaus Couple	18 x 12"	1995
151	Black Lady with Blue Hat	14 x 11"	1996

152	South African	15 x 11"	1998
153	Draining Lady	22 1/2" x 15"	1997
154	Self-portrait with Monkey Face	14 x 11"	1996
155	French Publisher	22 x 15"	1998
156	Baboon	30 x 22"	1986
	Collection: David Putnam		
157	Craig	15 x 11"	1998
158	Falling Man Mouth	18 x 12"	1995
	Collection: Catherine Chermayeff		
159	Lady at Sea	22 x 15"	1998
160	Cat Fur	18 1/2" x 15"	1999
161	Cat Face	30 x 22"	1990
	Collection: Private		
162	Movie Star	22" x 15"	1997
	Collection: Arthur & Barbara Dubow		
163	Airmail Mouth	15 x 11"	1998
	Collection: Maureen Kinney		
164	Round Head	15 x 11"	1998
165	Insect Man	22 x 15"	1998
166	Insect Lady	22 x 15"	1998
	Collection: Patrick McDonough		
167	The Meeting	15 x 11"	1999
168	Neptune	22 x 15"	1998
169	Woman with Pillbox Hat	30 x 22 1/2"	1997
170	Striped Baboon	30 x 22"	1987
	Collection: George Kravis		
171	Queen of Glue	15 x 11"	1998
172	Laundry Man with Miyawaki and the American Academy in Rome	30 x 22"	1990
	Collection: Private		
173	Rug Saleslady	30 x 22"	1994
174	Clown Face	30 x 22 1/2"	1993
	Collection: IDS		
175	Jumbo	15 x 11"	1998
176	Party Personage	15 x 11"	1998
177	Hartman	22 x 15"	1998
178	Figure with Windmill Hat	22 1/2 x 15"	1997
179	Stargazer	15 x 11"	1998
180	Man in Derby	11 x 14"	1995
	Collection: Albert Lindauer		
181	Man in Tux	22 x 15"	1998
	Collection: Rick Globus		
182	Mexican Lady	22 x 15"	1998

183	Total Designer	15 x 11"	1998
	Collection: Mary A. Kelly		
184	Sumo in Harvatska	22 x 14"	1999
185	Lady in Red Coat	30 x 19"	1997
	Collection: Ronald P. Stanton		
186	Grey Beard	22 1/2 x 15"	1998
187	Turk	22 x 15"	1998
	Collection: Hansuli Keller		
188	Alexandr	30 x 22"	1990
189	El Blondo	30 x 22"	1997
190	Man in Tux II	22 x 15"	1998
191	Red Bed	22 x 15"	1998
192	Fire Nose	15 x 11"	1997
	Collection: Karen Salsgiver		
193	English Lady	15 x 11"	1995
194	Greg's Robe	30 x 22"	1989
	Collection: Motoo Nakanishi		
195	German Lady in Japan	22 x 15"	1998
196	Johanna Mask	30 x 22"	1995
197	Tomato	30 x 22"	1993
	Collection: Watson Powell		
198	Michael Holden	22 x 13"	1995
199	Lady Mayor of Cadaques	15 x 11"	1998
200	Ruler Mouth	15 x 10"	1997
201	Running Man	22 x 15"	1998
202	George Bland	22 x 14"	1999
203	Grand Central Man	15 x 11"	1998
	Collection: Peter & Lois Charles		
204	Arapahoe Screamer	15 x 11"	1995
205	Apartment Head	22 x 15"	2000
206	Fifty-six	22 x 15"	2000
207	Doll	30 x 22 1/2"	1997
	Collection: Bruce & Susan Schunick Rubin		
208	Miro Personage with Top Hat	22 x 15"	1996
209	Ukak	24 1/2 x 21 1/2"	1992
210	Hong Kong Calligrapher	30 x 22"	1995
	Collection: Susan R. Witter		
211	James L.EGE	14 1/2 x 11 1/2"	1994
212	Passenger for Dieppe	30 x 22"	1992
	Collection: Pleasant Company		
213	Naked Astronaut	22 x 15"	1990
214	Swiss Lady	22 x 15"	1987
215	Girgenti Clown	15 x 10"	1997

216	Funny Nose	15 x 11"	1986
	Collection: Private		
217	Foot Nose	22 x 15"	2000
218	Bulgarian Comic	15 x 11"	2000
219	Hand	22 1/2 x 15"	2000
220	Ivan's X-ray	22 x 15"	2000
221	Lion from Wellfleet	30 x 22"	1986
	Collection: Private		
222	Cat's Paw	11 x 10"	1996
223	Tackle	47 x 35"	1999
	Iris Print		
224	Stray Cat	18 x 12"	1999
225	Alley Cat with Fish	16 x 11 1/2"	1999
226	Sylvia & Paul	15 x 22"	1993
227	North African	15 x 11"	1985
	Collection: Leo & Nora Lionni		
228	Post Mistress	15 x 11"	1998
229	Israeli Woodsman	15 x 11"	1998
230	Mexican Lover	15 x 11"	1987
	Collection: Maro Chermayeff		
231	Man in Uniform	23 x 16"	1999
232	Jay	22 x 15"	2000
233	Ziesing-Baur	22 x 15"	1997
234	Guide	30 x 22"	1995
235	#16 Blue Door Face	15 x 11"	1998
	Collection: Charmaine Donnelly		
236	Henry Hess, Taxpayer	15 x 13"	1999
237	Falconer	30 x 22"	1999
238	Parakeet Man with Red Cap	21 x 15"	1999
239	Hotel Doorman	30 x 22 1/2"	1993
240	Sandpiper	22 x 15"	2000
241	Colorado Butterfly	18 x 13"	1999
242	Colorado Ceskovenesko	30 x 22"	1999
243	Bar Prestida	30 x 22"	1999
244	Artist with Blue Goatee	22 x 15"	1995
245	Girl Face	22 1/2 x 15"	1997
246	German with White Beard	22 x 15"	2000
247	Swan Hair	15 x 10"	1997
	Collection: Meredith Brogan		
248	Brno Mechanic	30 x 22"	1998